Also by the Author

FLOATING
WALKING DISTANCE

These Things Happen

MARIAN THURM

POSEIDON PRESS
NEW YORK LONDON TORONTO SYDNEY TOKYO

Poseidon Press
Simon & Schuster Building
Rockefeller Center
1230 Avenue of the Americas
New York, New York 10020

POSEIDON PRESS is a registered trademark
of Simon & Schuster Inc.
POSEIDON PRESS colophon is a trademark
of Simon & Schuster Inc.

Designed by Gilda Hannah
Manufactured in the United States of America
10 9 8 7 6 5 4 3 2 1
Library of Congress Cataloging in Publication Data
Thurm, Marian.
  These things happen / Marian Thurm.
    p. cm.
  I. Title.
PS3570.H83T47 1988
813'.54–dc19   88-15586
ISBN 0-671-64924-8   CIP

"Lovers" first appeared in *The New Yorker;* "Leaving
Johanna" and "Snow-Child" (under a different title) in
Mademoiselle; "Ice" and "Sounds" (under a different
title and in different form) in *Ms.;* "Flying" in *Mississippi
Review;* "Squirrels" and "Away from the Heart" (under a
different title) in *The Boston Globe Magazine;* "Romance"
in *Fiction Network.*
(continued on page 174)

For Sam

Contents

Lovers

In a pancake house in Gainesville, Florida, Valerie and her mother are silently dividing up a copy of *The New York Times*. Generously, Valerie offers her mother the best section, the one with all the cultural news—the only news Marilyn cares about. In the three days that they have been on the road together, Valerie hasn't had many generous impulses. She wishes she were better company. Apologies and some sort of explanation are in order, but then she would have to open up her marriage to her mother, something she has never done. Her mother, though, is eager to share every small detail of her own current romance. Valerie's father died last year, and recently Marilyn has begun seeing a man whom she met at a Carnegie Hall concert. Joseph is Hungarian; during

9

the revolution, he somehow managed to get to Israel, and then to New York, where he found work as a diamond cutter. According to Marilyn, he is a man of great kindness and sensitivity. Like someone in love for the first time, she cannot stop talking about him, cannot stop herself from repeating the same details a hundred times over. Her eyes shine with unexpected happiness, even at seven-thirty in the morning, in a pancake house with dusty windows and sticky floors.

A middle-aged waitress approaches their table. In her short-sleeved white pants suit and white shoes, she looks like a dental technician.

"I can't make up my mind," Marilyn says, smiling at her. "What do you recommend?"

"French toast, eggs, I don't know. It's up to you."

Very quietly, Valerie orders an ice-cream soda.

Marilyn looks to the waitress for sympathy.

"Ketchup on French toast, Cheerios soaking in a bowl of Pepsi-Cola, I've seen it all," the waitress says. "If this young lady wants ice cream for breakfast, that's just fine with me."

"Thank you," Valerie says, and grabs the best section of the paper back from her mother. "Would it be possible to have us out of here in ten minutes?"

Marilyn explains to the waitress that they are from New York, where people are always in a hurry, even if they don't have anywhere special to go. In fact, the two of them are on their way down to Hollywood, where Valerie's grandfather lives in a mouse-sized house by himself. "He's extremely independent," Marilyn says, "but lately in the middle of the night he's been waking up with sharp pains in his chest, and no matter how many times the doctors in the emergency room tell him it's only indigestion he doesn't believe them. They tell him not to eat just before going to bed, to eat a light dinner in the early evening and then nothing more until breakfast."

"Got it," says the waitress.

"Every now and then," Marilyn says, "a doctor will surprise you and say something that actually makes sense. I was married to one for a thousand years, and I have to tell you that most of the things he said had to be taken with a grain of salt."

This is the perfect moment for Valerie to excuse herself from the table and make a phone call home. The phones are directly outside the rest rooms, and it's a struggle to hear the operator's instructions. Nick doesn't answer. After twenty-one rings, Valerie hangs up, deciding he's in the shower or on the subway headed for work. But immediately this strikes her as too uncomplicated, too unsatisfying. (The farther she travels from Nick, the more fully her pessimism blooms.) She decides he's gone to see his ex-wife, with whom he says he still feels a tenuous connection. His ex-wife is small and pretty, but not very perceptive. "I don't understand how we can be breaking up when we've just picked out new things for the bedroom," she had told Nick when he said that their marriage was over. They'd ordered several thousand dollars' worth of furniture—an antique armoire, a brass headboard, a chaise longue—and Nick left her anyway, even though he had to admit the bedroom would look terrific.

He and Valerie have been married for almost two years. Valerie works as a loan officer in a bank, and Nick teaches anatomy to first-year medical students. Nick is exceptionally confident, the kind of person who can make Valerie feel uneasy by the arch of his eyebrows, the slightest trace of mockery in his voice. She's vulnerable in his presence, never knowing when he's going to challenge her or prove her wrong—something he rarely attempted before their marriage. Usually it's a simple thing, like keeping the Cornish hens in the oven too long, or choosing wallpaper that clashes with the print of their shower curtain. She makes mistakes like these nearly every day. Even more painful are the times when Nick speaks to her as if she were a child who hadn't done her homework carefully. Where did you see *that,* he'd ask after hearing her say that in some cities in Poland waiting lists for apartments are eighteen years long, or that the average M.D. dies at the age of fifty-six. He'd insist that she hadn't read the newspaper article as thoroughly as she should have or had not thought things through properly. (Working as she does in the bank, she knows all about weighing the facts, she wants to say, but it seems too obvious to mention.) That's the scientist in Nick, she tells herself; accuracy and precision are what he's after. But often she has to remind him that school is over for the day, that in any case she isn't one of his students, and that he sounds like a jackass when he talks to her like that. And then he apologizes and says he hadn't meant it that way at all. She can't help feeling, though, that their life together is becoming an endless round of accusations and reluctant apologies.

This seems intolerable to her. She has always been a romantic, always believed in love, long-term and sustaining, something that would see her through a lifetime. But when she told this to a psychologist she went to see once or twice when things got bad with Nick, he looked at her mournfully and said, "You and a cast of millions. What else is new?"

Surprisingly, Nick, too, considers himself a romantic: He's saved the ticket stubs from all the movies they've seen together, and the matchbooks from every restaurant they've eaten in, collecting and storing them like treasures in the inlaid-rosewood box that Valerie gave him for his birthday. (Is there a similar collection documenting his first marriage, she wonders.) On her thirtieth birthday this year, he locked himself away in the kitchen for hours, emerging at midnight with a braided loaf of sourdough bread, each braid dyed a different, brilliant color. He took snapshots of a slice of it carefully arranged on a white linen napkin: evidence of the lengths he had gone to please her.

Now and then, Nick meets his ex-wife for lunch—just to see how she's getting along, he claims. He is very casual about these meetings. He sometimes forgets to mention them to Valerie for several days. "Seeing her means more to you than it does to me," he said to Valerie in a soothing voice the night before she left for Florida. She shook her head, reassured of nothing. "What you need," he went on quietly, "is someone without any past at all, a goddamn blank piece of paper." No, she wanted to say; what she needed was someone easier, softer, more patient. When she left the next morning, they kissed for a long while. Finally, she had to pull away. "It's only a couple of weeks," she said, smiling. "I'll be back before you know it." But it hadn't felt like the truth to her; she'd blushed as soon as the words were spoken.

Sitting opposite her mother now, Valerie watches Marilyn write out a postcard to Joseph with a pink felt-tip pen. "Can I read this to you?" Marilyn asks, and she begins reading before Valerie has a chance to answer. "What do you think? Is it too much to say that I miss him terribly? I said something to that effect in yesterday's card, too. This is just a rough draft anyway." Marilyn reaches into a suede handbag and shows Valerie the pile of postcards she's taken from the motel they stayed in the night before. "These are some other versions—some are a little more restrained than others, if you know what I mean," she says.

Valerie sips at her ice-cream soda, which is warm and slightly bitter.

"What a terrible face on you," Marilyn says. "Am I supposed to take that face personally or are you just mad at the world?"

Valerie gazes out into the parking lot, where a broad-shouldered woman is dragging a small, weeping child from the front of a van. The van has a heart-shaped rear window on one side and a tear-shaped one on the other. "We should have made more of an effort to get plane reservations," Valerie says. "It's crazy to be taking the car this distance."

Shuffling her stack of postcards, Marilyn says, "Too bad Grandpa couldn't have chosen a better time to fly into a panic. This time of year, everyone in the world wants to go to Florida. He sounded so pitiful on the phone last week, after he'd gotten back from the hospital. Whenever I think about that conversation, I'm convinced this trip was absolutely unavoidable." She picks out a postcard, holds it up to the fluorescent lighting overhead, and smiles. "Now, here's one any man would be delighted to find in his mailbox."

"Let me see," Valerie says.

"No," says her mother. "Not this one. This one's strictly personal and confidential." She raises her arm higher and waves the postcard in the air. Valerie is out of her seat, standing on her toes, the backs of her knees painfully stretched, when her mother's arm swoops down suddenly and she tears the postcard into tiny pieces that drift to the floor. "You never listen to anything I say about Joseph," Marilyn says. "You tap your foot, stare at the ceiling, anything to avoid paying attention. When are you going to tell me what I'm doing wrong?" When Valerie remains silent, her mother says, "You'll have to excuse me if my happiness comes at an inconvenient time for you."

"It's not anything you're doing wrong," Valerie says at last. "It's only me."

"You," her mother murmurs. "Every day, in the car, I look at you for hints of something—anything. But you're only listening to the rock and roll on the radio, pretending there's no one in the seat next to you, that you're traveling all these hours and all these miles alone."

Valerie's grandfather, Willy, lives in a house of peach-colored stucco, set on a tiny lawn of yellowish grass. The rooms are furnished with aluminum-and-plastic beach furniture, and there's a fine, powdery dust everywhere, even across the TV screen. Assessing the hours of house-cleaning before her, Marilyn perks up immediately.

"You can't believe what the bathroom looks like," she confides to Valerie. "You just want to run right out the minute you get in there."

"Sad," says Valerie, who assumes her grandfather is losing his eyesight.

"Sad?" Marilyn is in the utility room off the kitchen, looking for a broom. "Your grandfather was never much of a housekeeper, if you really want to know. He always liked everything neat—magazines in a nice even pile, beds made with perfect hospital corners—but he never went in much for sweeping and dusting."

"True to form," Willy says, joining Valerie at the kitchen table. "She's in my house five minutes and already she's passing judgment."

"Why should I be surprised that a man who doesn't believe in sweeping wouldn't have a broom?" Marilyn says. "How about a sponge?"

Valerie touches her grandfather's smooth, narrow wrist. "Tell me how you've been. Have you been eating?" she asks. At the end of last summer, Willy's brother, Norman, who had shared the house with him, struck up a conversation with a woman on a bench in a shopping mall. A few weeks later, he married her. Willy refused to attend the wedding, and hasn't spoken to Norman since. According to Willy, his new sister-in-law isn't "a high-quality person." He can't understand how Norman could have married a woman who has dyed red hair and wears perfume so strong it lingers in the house for hours after she's gone.

"I eat, I sleep; I'm surviving," Willy says.

"You miss the company, I bet."

"Never," Willy says. "I've got plenty of company. In fact, I'm surprised my pals haven't been over yet today."

Marilyn is squatting on the floor, sponging down the linoleum with Mr. Clean. Through an open window, a neighbor's television can be heard perfectly.

"So how's your new boyfriend?" Willy says, frowning at the top of Marilyn's curly gray head. "Is he going to marry you?"

"What? When did I ever say one word about marriage? Not that I don't fantasize about it occasionally." Marilyn has eased her way under the table and is crouched there, moving a sponge dreamily across the speckled linoleum.

"That's my foot, in case you're interested," says Valerie.

"Marriage," Willy says mournfully. "It comes when you least expect it. You walk over to the mall intending to do a little shopping, and there it is, waiting for you right outside Drug World." From his seat, he kicks a cabinet door closed with one foot. "That weasel. She was sitting there reading *Crime and Punishment,* trying to pass herself off as an intellectual. 'Tolstoy,' my brother says, and smiles at her with those big white false teeth."

"Dostoyevski," Marilyn calls from under the table.

"Yeah, well, the weasel was too lovesick to correct him. In two seconds, she and Norman were across the mall at Baskin-Robbins, enjoying an ice-cream cone. And there I was, sitting on that bench like a big dope, waiting for the two of them to come back. I read twenty pages of *Crime and Punishment* before I realized they'd forgotten all about me."

"It must have been awful," Valerie says, and puts her arms around her grandfather's neck.

"So I stole the weasel's book. I took it home with me and read every last page. Then I mailed it back. They were already married by then, living in that dark little apartment of hers that you have to travel across a cat-walk to get into. Sometimes," Willy says, his voice a whisper, "I imagine them in the wind and the rain, crossing the catwalk, huddled against each other."

"Kind of romantic, if you think about it," says Marilyn, and crawls out from under the table. Her face is flushed and sweaty, her pinkish eye shadow smudged over the bridge of her nose. "The wind and the rain, the two of them—"

"Soaking wet," Willy says. "Soaked to the bone. Their clothes have to be dry-cleaned. It costs them a fortune."

Valerie laughs and shakes her head. Her grandfather is unforgiving and unyielding in ways she almost admires. Forty-five years ago, he divorced his wife after she admitted she had a habit of being unfaithful to him. He never remarried, and raised their three children on his own. Not a happy life, or an easy one, but simply the best he could manage. Valerie is thinking of Nick and wondering why she had to fall for someone who makes her feel so unsure of herself, so helpless. Over the years, friends have confided in her, come to her for advice and gone away satisfied. She has always seen through other people's lives with a clarity that eludes her when she examines her own. Eyes open, she imagines Nick's soft-skinned, boyish hands kneading dough, remembers the velvety dust of flour that settled across his dark brow, the look of pleasure about his eyes and mouth as he sliced into the neon colors of her birthday bread.

She tells her grandfather that she'd like to use the phone.

"Not today," Willy says. "I haven't had a dial tone all day. Someone from the phone company was supposed to come by this afternoon, but don't hold your breath."

"I should call Joseph," Marilyn says. "Or maybe I shouldn't."

The doorbell rings—a startling electronic buzz. "Come in, come in," Willy yells, and a young Indian woman in a sari and a little boy walk through the side door into the kitchen, a Teddy bear between them, each of them holding one of its paws. Willy smiles as he introduces the visitors. "This is Meera, my newest granddaughter, and this is Shahed, my one and only great-grandson."

"Your what?" Marilyn says. She's standing on a wrought-iron chair with a feather duster in her hand, swiping at cobwebs in a corner of the ceiling.

"I have no one in America to talk to except Grandpa," says Meera. "No one." She's a beautiful woman, with a diamond chip decorating the curve of one nostril. Her bare feet are beautiful, too: dark, slender feet, the nails polished bright red.

"Grandpa," Shahed says. There's a thin silver bracelet around each of his wrists. He's wearing a T-shirt with Sesame Street characters on it; across the front is printed "Lunch Is My Favorite Subject."

"My Florida family," Willy says, looking pleased with himself. "And this is my New York family."

"Aren't you lucky," Marilyn says coolly.

"Meera and Shahed are Muslims," Willy says. "They're very religious people. Meera's husband is a psychologist."

"No, no," Meera says. "Psychiatrist."

"Whatever. They moved in next door a few months ago, just before Norman went off with the weasel."

"The weasel has orange hair like a carrot," Meera says,

as if this were a line she has memorized. Then she laughs and covers her mouth with her hand. Valerie shoots her a sympathetic look. She wants to make up for Marilyn's coldness, to signal to Meera that her mother's disapproval should not be taken to heart. Willy likes to collect honorary families that he can rave about long-distance to Marilyn; mostly, Valerie thinks, because he knows just how much it hurts her to hear it. Marilyn, who is the only daughter among his three children, is the one who worries most about him. But she has never been able to please him; face-to-face or long-distance, the air between them bristles with discontent. Once, she told Valerie, "If he were a lover whose attention I was dying for, I'd flirt like crazy, say something provocative, spray perfume all over my hair —anything to get noticed. But of course he's only my father." She shrugged her shoulders and gave Valerie a sad half-smile. And yet here was her mother battling cobwebs as if it mattered, as if there were always the possibility that something she did or said might turn out to be the right thing after all.

Valerie gazes straight into Willy's bleached-looking blue eyes. Who is Willy that he can afford to turn down love when it is offered him? He appears to be nothing more than a fragile old man, small and thin as a boy. Valerie would like to shake him hard and see the confusion in his startled face.

She climbs up next to her mother on the chair and takes the duster from her hand. "Stop trying so hard," Valerie whispers.

Tears shimmer in her mother's eyes. "What could be easier?" Marilyn says.

Willy has taken Shahed onto his lap, and is stroking the little boy's cheek with two fingers. "Sweet boy," he says. "But why can't you ever wear shoes? Your feet will get hard like an old man's."

Giggling, Meera says, "Sometimes I take your advice, sometimes not."

Willy says, "I told you to keep your car in the garage—begged you, practically. I knew they would steal it." To Valerie and her mother he explains, "It was brand-new, a shined-up Volkswagen something or other. The one week she had it, Meera and I drove to some new malls and every day to the beach. We sat in the sand on a bedspread with Shahed and watched the sea gulls. I don't mind telling you the beach usually makes me feel lonely, but this particular week was perfect—day after day of unclouded skies and water the color of turquoise stones."

"Perfect," Meera says, her head bowed. Everyone is silent, contemplating the word. "My husband is never home," Meera says, and then in a loud voice, "It's not a life. Who can live this life? I want him to be sorry, to apologize—something."

"There are some people," says Willy, "who can't apologize for anything. Can't or won't or don't know how."

"Are you talking to me?" Marilyn asks. "Was that an apology drifting in my direction?"

"That was probably just a statement about people in general. And what would I be apologizing for, anyway?" Willy says. He kisses the side of Shahed's neck, and Shahed starts to slide off his lap. Willy pulls him back at first, then, sighing, lets him go.

There's a rustling at the back of the house, behind the screened-in porch, where everyone is slouched in lawn chairs, watching the end of the eleven o'clock news. Valerie stands up and presses her face against the screen. A figure dressed in light-colored clothes waves to her.

"Is that Valerie?" the figure asks. "Don't you recognize me?"

Willy comes up next to the screen beside her. "Ah," he says. "The bridegroom returns."

"May I come in?" Norman says.

"What for?"

"I tried calling, but your phone was out of order."

"And?" Willy says. "Go on."

"It's kind of nippy out here. I forgot to bring a jacket. Aren't you going to let me in?"

"I like having this screen between us," Willy says. "It's as if you're in some kind of prison and I'm here on the outside. But of course we can always pass messages back and forth."

Norman knocks on the screen with his fist. "She kicked me out, Willy. I have no place to sleep tonight."

"The weasel?" Willy says. "The phony-baloney intellectual who swept you off your feet right in the middle of the mall?"

Marilyn jumps up and grabs Willy's arm. "Will you stop torturing him, please?"

"Hi, Marilyn," Norman says. "Nice to see you again, even under circumstances as unpleasant as these."

Valerie, at a signal from her mother, darts into the kitchen. "The door's unlocked now," she calls to Norman, and leans out into the darkness. It's cool outside, just as Norman said, but also very humid. At her feet, a slug drags itself along the concrete stoop, then disappears into the glistening ragged grass of Willy's yard. There's a light on in Meera's kitchen, next door, and laughter from her television set drifts over the unpainted picket fence that separates the two houses. If Valerie were home now, she and Nick would be sitting side by side in bed, books on their laps, their bare feet occasionally touching. She would slip down along the mattress, rest her head on Nick's chest, and press her ear against his heart, listening for secrets. Funny that you could live with someone for months, even years, and still be astonished at what he was really thinking. Like Nick's first wife, when she found out she'd mistaken a roomful of new furniture for proof that the love between them was secure. And Nick himself, who has no idea that what continues to draw Valerie to him is the faint, ordinary perfume of his hair, his smooth, long-fingered hands, and the slope of his shoulders when he's tired. If she were never to see him again, those are the things that would haunt her the most.

"Valerie, my savior," she hears Norman say. He throws his arm across her shoulders and together they walk into the house. Norman is all in white, very dapper, with a full head of hair and a thin, elegantly groomed mustache. He carries a paper sack that says "Nathan's Famous" on it. "For you," he says, offering her the bag. "For you, who gave me sanctuary." Then he winks at her, just to let her know he's only half serious.

Valerie opens the bag and empties the contents onto the table: two ears of corn, two eggrolls, and two slices of partially eaten pizza wrapped in grease-stained wax paper.

"A romantic dinner for two, as you can see," Norman says. "Unfortunately, the romance has gone from my marriage."

Marilyn and Willy have joined them in the kitchen, where they study the food on the table with their hands behind their backs.

"Jesus," says Willy. "You're breaking my heart."

"You just ignore your baby brother," Marilyn tells Norman. "He's exceptionally cranky today."

"What do you know? You don't know anything about it," Willy says.

"I'm here to pick up the pieces of my shattered life," says Norman. He picks up an eggroll and holds it at arm's length. He frowns, as if he were examining it for flaws, then drops it back onto the table.

"So she's through with you," Willy says. "Big deal. People discard each other every day of the week."

"That may be," Norman says, "but this is something new—a marriage down the drain because of a sharp little noise. Did you know my teeth click when I eat? We were in Nathan's, having dinner, when all of a sudden she looked at me in a very unfriendly way and said, 'I'm going to scream; my patience is gone. I can't live with that noise anymore. I can't live with *you* anymore.'"

"Life is full of surprises, even at this late date," Norman says. Pressing two fingers against each temple, he closes his eyes. It's as if he were listening for ghosts or reading minds, attempting miracles of one sort or another. They all watch him, waiting to hear what he's discovered. "Love," he says finally. And then, the next moment, "Damn it all to hell."

Valerie and her mother are preparing for bed in what used to be Norman's room; Willy and Norman are in the master bedroom, across the hall. Marilyn is already in her bed, wiggling around under the sheet as Valerie undresses and shuts off the lamp on the night table between them.

"Joseph," Marilyn says, and sighs out loud. "I feel so privileged sometimes." Valerie has to smile.

"Sweetie pie?" her mother says.

"Me? I'm here."

"When I first met him, that night at the concert, we ducked into a coffee shop—just to escape the rain, really. He told me all about his life, how hard it had been to start over, how afraid he'd been. He trusted me, for God knows what reason. It was wonderful to be regarded that way, to be the kind of person someone would tell his whole life to."

Valerie is on her stomach, her head tucked into the curve of her arm. Her mother's quiet, careful voice is putting her to sleep, as if she were a child again, listening to some beloved, comforting story about imaginary people.

"Sometimes it's easier to talk in the dark," her mother says.

This is the last thing Valerie hears before falling asleep. In her grandfather's house, in a narrow, unfamiliar bed, she dreams pleasantly of Nick. Arms linked, they're floating above a city street, drifting like balloons high above the pavement; people smile up at them. "Lovers," a man says knowingly. Nick is a calmer, sweeter version of himself, the way Valerie remembers him during the early months of their marriage. In the dream, even his voice is softer; it's a voice she could listen to forever, even though his words are indistinct and impossible to follow as she and Nick descend slowly to earth.

"Valerie," someone is saying close to her ear. "I need your help."

"So you want to know when he stopped making me happy," Valerie says to herself, or maybe aloud; she can't tell which.

"Are you awake?" her mother says. The light from the lamp on the night table is unbearably bright.

"Why are we up so early?" Valerie asks.

"Those two nuts heated up the eggrolls and the rest of that junk."

"For breakfast?"

"I'm talking about a midnight snack. They sneaked out of bed, ate everything in sight, and went back to sleep. Now Grandpa insists he's dying."

"And you want me to drive him to the hospital."

Marilyn tips her head back and yawns. She straightens her shoulders. "He's not going anywhere. All he needs is some Di-Gel and he'll be all set."

"That's what you're going to say to a man who thinks he's dying?"

On the other side of the hall, Willy moans. Valerie hurries into her grandfather's room, her mother behind her. Norman greets them from a lawn chair, dressed only in his white pants. "I was too hungry to sleep," he explains, "and Willy was kind enough to keep me company."

Willy is in bed, flat on his back, his eyes closed. "It's all true," he says. "Even at the moment you know your life is lost, there's time to travel through it again." Abruptly, he sits up very straight. "There I am! I'm in knickers and argyle socks on the stoop in front of the building we lived in on Lexington Avenue. It was a lovely neighborhood, though I guess it's been Spanish Harlem for years and years now. Anyway, there I am, shooting the breeze with my buddies—"

"It was never what anyone would call lovely," Norman says. "Shame on you. I thought dying men told the truth."

Willy massages his chest, then moves his hand toward his middle. "Get out of my room," he says. "Get out of my house. Go home to your wife."

Rising slowly from his chair, Norman says, "Take the medication Marilyn has for you. Don't be so stubborn."

Marilyn approaches her father and sits at the edge of his bed. In her palm are two cellophane-wrapped tablets. "You don't even need water," she says. "You just put them in your mouth and chew them up."

"Get off my deathbed, please."

Marilyn is already off the bed. "I'm going back to sleep. Wake me up if you need me."

"I need you *now*. Don't leave."

"There's always me," Valerie says. "I'm not going anywhere." Her hand closes around the little cellophane package her mother passes to her on her way out the door.

Valerie sits in the webbed green-and-yellow chair at the foot of her grandfather's bed and rubs her eyes.

"Come closer," Willy says.

She's at his side, slipping the medication into his mouth. "Chew," she says, and Willy obeys.

Gradually the room lightens; a garbage truck groans outside, a telephone rings in a neighbor's house. From a straw mat on the floor, Valerie keeps watch as her grandfather sleeps, propped up against the carved wooden headboard that had been a wedding gift from Norman nearly sixty years ago. Then suddenly Willy's eyes open wide. He pulls the sheet over his head until he has disappeared beneath it, a motionless figure shrouded in white, a child's idea of a ghost.

"In truth," he says, "the weasel, Doris Feldmann, was very beautiful. Tall and thin, graceful even in the way she sat, the way she held a book in her hands. I sat down next to her on the bench almost as soon as I saw her, but my tongue felt fuzzy in my mouth, and I couldn't say a word. Nothing. And even if I could have, what would have happened? Sooner or later, she would have noticed that my teeth click as bad as Norman's."

Valerie nods her head, but she's no longer listening. She and Nick are at a crowded party in a loft in Soho, about to meet for the first time. Nick is stretched out on the floor reading a magazine, oblivious of everyone above him. Valerie hasn't noticed him yet, and at first, when he cries out in pain, she does nothing at all. She's standing on his fingers, crushing them, he yells up from the floor. Together, they rush to the kitchen, and neither of them says a word as Nick holds his hand under a stream of cold water. When finally he pulls away from the faucet, Valerie bends forward and kisses this stranger's hand without hesitation, utterly amazed, only a moment later, at what she has done.

Sanctuary

~~~~~~~~~~~~~~~~~~~~~~~~~~~

Arriving at the bar mitzvah over two hours late, Tuck ignored his lover's sigh as he settled into a crushed velvet seat near the front of the sanctuary, directly behind Andrew. He studied the pale, immaculate skin at the back of his lover's neck, the narrow, elegant ears, the long gray-blond hair tied back neatly with a strip of black suede in honor of the occasion. Brian, the bar mitzvah boy, was chanting his portion of the Torah in a trembly voice, and Tuck could feel his body go tense in sympathy. He folded one hand into a fist and brought it to his mouth, giving himself a series of short, quick punches. Turning his head slightly to the left and right, he picked out familiar profiles—Andrew's mother and father and sister, seated to one side of him, and Cynthia, Andrew's ex-wife, seated at the other. After the ceremony, Tuck thought, he would nod, and smile at them graciously, offering his congratulations and shaking hands all around. And that would be that. He hadn't much to say to these people, who were probably wishing he would do them a favor and disappear off the face of the earth. Certainly this was true of Andrew's mother, a small, straight-backed senior citizen whose hair, he noticed, had somehow turned an extraordinary pinkish orange that happened to match her wool suit perfectly. Two years ago, upon learning that Andrew and Tuck were lovers, she fell into a swoon and could not stop asking, over and over: How could this have happened to me? Cynthia, who at the time had already been divorced from Andrew for more than a year, had taken the news almost as hard, saying she could never have imagined what it would be like to feel so utterly humiliated and unloved. Her darkest thoughts centered on Tuck, and for a long time she would freeze in his presence and at the sound of his voice over the phone. She and Tuck had only recently begun to exchange more than their usual pained two-word conversations, but it appeared unlikely that they would ever make that broad leap toward friendship. Oddly, it was Tuck she had never completely forgiven, though she and Andrew had progressed to a reasonable level of compassion and understanding.

The fact that he'd shown up at all—two hours late or not—at Andrew's son's bar mitzvah made him smile to himself. He was braver than he thought, as courageous as Brian, who had hit his stride following the reading of the Torah, and was singing his heart out. Now the rabbi was calling for Andrew and Cynthia to stand before the congregation and repeat a prayer aloud. They rose together from their seats and Tuck watched as Cynthia's hand reached, without hesitation, for Andrew's. There was a rustling in the sanctuary: People shifting in their

seats, rearranging purses in their laps, whispering in uni-
son, it seemed. "What a farce," Tuck heard a voice close
by saying. Andrew and Cynthia sank back down into
their chairs and the rabbi slipped an arm around Brian
and delivered a quick little speech about the meaning
this day would always hold for him. Good sweet boy that
he was, Brian looked directly into the rabbi's broad,
gleaming face and nodded appreciatively. Tuck remembered himself at thirteen; God, what a mess. He'd been a
tall, bony, argumentative kid who could not keep his
mouth shut in school. He drove his teachers wild, asking
too many questions that they were either unwilling or
unable to answer. He was too arrogant to have a lot of
friends, but later, at Yale, surrounded by so many
equally bright, capable students, he lost his swagger. He
fell in love with art history and went straight to graduate
school after college, then taught at Columbia and N.Y.U.
It wasn't until he moved to London on his sabbatical and
met Andrew that he could say with certainty that love
had finally come his way. Andrew was older, twice divorced, and had a thick gray beard that Tuck found irresistible. Following Andrew home to New York at the end
of his academic leave, Tuck gave himself over fully to
their life together. He encouraged Andrew to move into
his apartment on the upper West Side, and they soon
bought a weekend house in Connecticut, which was just
an hour's drive from the fanciful gift shop that Andrew
had owned since his second divorce. Entering the store
for the first time, Tuck had moved slowly about the
crowded room as if he were in a trance. A five-foot-tall,
foam rubber and papier-mâché pig dressed as a grocer
in a white coat and straw hat presided over a table covered with baskets of silk vegetables—tomatoes, radishes,
celery, asparagus, mushrooms. A real tree, silk peaches
fastened with string to its branches, stood in a corner.
Brooms and chairs hung on pegs placed high on the

wall, and there were three oak hutches cluttered with hand-painted dishes. Tables beautifully set with pink-and-green china and linen were randomly positioned about the room; everything was clean and bright and for sale, except, Andrew said, the pig, which was a gift from an old friend. Tuck continued to wander through the store, stopping to run his hands over the silk stalks of celery, the smooth surface of a large ceramic goose with a checked wool scarf around its neck, a basket full of carved wooden croissants and *baguettes*. He felt an urgent, inexplicable need to touch everything, as if the texture of Andrew's life were perceptible beneath his fingertips.

He finished out the semester at school and that summer gave up both his job and the apartment in the city. He and Andrew moved into their small, drafty country house, and became business partners. Early every morning, as Andrew drove them to work, Tuck half-dozed in the front seat of their flashy black Toyota Supra, and was reminded that he had done well in altering his life so radically. He loved the slow-moving hours at the shop, the genteel housewives who picked carefully through his wares, settling with satisfaction on place mats and napkins for eight at a cost of two hundred dollars, often insisting that the store was the loveliest they had ever seen. It was a women's store, really; men seldom came in, but when they did, they'd see their mistake immediately and disappear murmuring apologies. In between customers, Andrew and Tuck talked endlessly, some of it business, but most of it about how disappointing their lives had been before they'd met and how well everything seemed to be turning out now. Brian stayed with them two weekends a month and Tuck enjoyed his good-natured company, enjoyed fixing him meals his mother would never have allowed him to have—Pac-Man pasta straight from the can, platefuls of burned bacon, potato chip–and–cream cheese sandwiches. If Tuck had ever conjured a child (and he had wished for one from time to time), Brian would have been just what he had in mind. Cynthia, of course, was another story. According to Andrew, she was actually capable of great generosity, someone who had bent over backward trying to make him happy. She'll come around, Andrew kept promising. One day she'll speak to you like a normal person and all those bad vibes will fade away. "Right," Tuck said, rolling his eyes. He had no choice but to live with it: each brief, chilly conversation, iced over with Cynthia's bitterness.

The congregation rose now as the rabbi swept past them down the center aisle in his black floor-length gown, followed by the cantor, the bar mitzvah boy, and the president of the temple, then rows of worshipers and guests. In the crowded aisle, Tuck shook hands with Andrew's family and congratulated them one by one.

"What a ceremony," he said as he let go of Andrew's father's hand. "The music, I mean the singing, was so lovely and sad."

"What do you mean, sad?" said Andrew's mother. "This is supposed to be a joyous occasion, mister."

"He means melancholy and he's right," Cynthia said. She winked at Tuck. "And that's the end of that, okay?"

"Absolutely," said Andrew, and gestured for the family to proceed down the aisle in front of him. "Where were you?" he whispered to Tuck.

"In the parking lot, smoking too many cigarettes, trying to work up the courage to come inside."

Andrew frowned at this, but all he said was, "You'll get through it; it's going to be fine."

"I'll bet," said Tuck. Daringly, he ran a finger along the suede at the back of his lover's hair. "Brian did great," he said.

"I was a nervous wreck," Andrew told him. "Between

your not showing up and *his* shaky voice, I thought I was going to have heart failure."

"Imagine how *I* felt."

"They're not going to bite you," Andrew said, and laughed. "But if they do, feel free to bite back."

"Thanks a lot," said Tuck.

The sanctuary had nearly emptied out; at its foot, beyond a wide set of folding doors, was the collation—two long tables draped in white paper and filled with plates of sponge cake, cookies, and bottles of wine and soda. Little boys in miniature suits and girls in party dresses and tights slammed into each other deliberately and dived under the tables, shrieking. In a stroller, his chest covered with a bib that resembled a tuxedo, a baby slept with his head in his hands, looking stricken. Tuck and Andrew separated; Andrew going off to greet his guests, leaving Tuck to fend for himself. Aside from the family, there was no one he knew, no one for him to talk to, really. This was only the beginning of what would surely be an impossibly long day: After the collation, the invited guests would move to a grander room in the temple, where there would be a live band, and hors d'oeuvres carried on silver trays by waiters in gold uniforms, and, finally, an endless buffet. Already feeling bereft, Tuck approached one of the tables and poured himself a paper cupful of unbearably sweet wine. He made a face as he swallowed it, then filled the cup with club soda, which he drank in sips. Next to him, two well-dressed women his age were having a conversation in voices pitched high above the noise that rose all around them.

"I'm selling Unicef greeting cards over the phone," one of them told the other, "and I'm not making any headway at all. My first three calls there was no one home, and the fourth was like, unbelievable. The woman who answered said, 'I don't buy or send cards, not since my daughter died. She was just sitting there stopped at a red light and along came some eighty-year-old who lost control of his car and killed her. Twenty-eight years old. So the only cards I send are birthday cards to my poor grandchildren, my daughter's three little boys.' Then the woman starts to cry. And I'm like, is this really happening?"

"What a bummer," said the woman's friend.

"I'm like, give me a break, I'm only trying to raise a little money for a worthy cause. She gave me goose bumps, and all of a sudden, she had me crying, too."

Unaccountably, tears sprang to Tuck's eyes. He rushed away from the table and out into the lobby, where he looked around frantically for the men's room. As soon as he found it, he locked himself inside a stall and pressed sheets of toilet tissue hard against his eyes. "Chill out," he said in a whisper. "Take it nice and easy." He wished he were back at the store, surrounded by cheerful clutter. The store was where he was most serene, especially on Wednesdays, Andrew's day off. Over the past few months, he'd looked forward keenly to his day alone, to the utter solitude—even the customers seemed an intrusion. Usually he read and smoked cigarettes and made calls to friends; once, just two weeks ago, he called an ex-lover named Denny, whom he hadn't spoken to in years. The following Wednesday, Denny took the train up to see him, though he was living with a member of the chorus of *Me and My Girl* and was, he'd told Tuck over the phone, as happy as he had ever been. "Good for you," Tuck said, surprised to hear how annoyed his own voice had sounded. When Denny arrived with a box lunch of saga blue, fancy crackers and a bottle of wine, Tuck found himself too unnerved to eat. He watched as Denny sliced into the cheese and spread it meticulously over one cracker after another. Tuck wanted to tell him what it was like to spend twenty-four hours of almost every day with your lover, and how, after a couple of years together, there were things your lover might say or do that would grate so sharply against your nerves, it would make your teeth hurt just to be in his company. But he kept silent and waited until Denny had finished his meal, then closed the store for the afternoon. He led Denny upstairs to the storeroom, where, among the cartons of china and linen, silk vegetables and Christmas decorations, they undressed on a thin flannel blanket laid against the floorboards. The encounter left him both soothed and excited, thrilled at the thought that falling in love was still, was always, a possibility, though certainly not with Denny, who would soon be catching a train back to his chorus boy. In the days that had passed since then, he'd gone over the facts a hundred times and more: He could not bear to give up his share of the shop and Andrew would certainly never give up his. He would sell back his half of the house in a minute, but Andrew could not possibly afford it. And so he had nowhere to go but home every night, nowhere to work and eat and sleep except beside Andrew. Their lives were as tightly bound to each other's as any two lives could be: Sometimes, in his worst moments, arguing with Andrew over what to make for dinner, or what day they had last changed the linens, or who was going to get out of bed to turn off the stereo, Tuck had to admit that all of it was intolerable, and that he was, without question, a man who was meant to live entirely alone. But other times, watching Andrew arrange things so delicately, so artfully, in the store, or sitting together in front of the fire in their living room, his fingers stroking Andrew's beard, he was contented, and knew he was exactly where he needed to be.

He listened now to a voice beyond his door saying, "Believe it, the marriage plans went straight down the sewer because the bride wanted to hear a Grateful Dead song when she walked down the aisle, and the groom just couldn't hack it."

Smiling as he emerged from the stall and headed toward a row of shining sinks, Tuck splashed water on his face and dried himself off with a handful of rough brown paper towels. The only other people in the room were a pair of mimes, a man and a woman in black leotards. The woman was putting makeup on her partner, drawing a red tear on his powdered cheekbone, smoothing shadow along the arch of his eyebrows while the man stared at nothing, patiently smoking a cigarette.

"Are you here for the bar mitzvah?" Tuck asked.

"We'll go anywhere for money," the man said. "Can't you see we're desperate?"

"Cut it out, Gerard," said his partner. "Do you want me to finish your makeup or not?"

"Well, good luck," Tuck offered, and went back out into the lobby, where he stopped to study an enormous oil painting entitled *The Tree of Life*. The leaves on the lowest branches were green, the ones above them silver, and the ones at the very top, gold. Every leaf—and there must have been hundreds—had a first and last name painted across it, and Tuck assumed that what he was looking at was a family history of sorts, of the congregation. And then out of nowhere came the clatter of high heels against linoleum tile, and there he was, side by side with Cynthia, who, he realized, looked spectacular in her black mini skirt and patterned black stockings.

"Need some help?" she asked, as if she were a saleswoman and Tuck a bewildered customer. "The greens are worth fifty dollars, the silver a hundred dollars, the gold, five hundred."

"Of course," said Tuck. "I had it all figured out." He heard himself laughing, but his hands were clammy and he could feel his heart pounding beneath his shirt pocket.

"You look terrible," said Cynthia in a friendly way.

He gazed down at his brass-buttoned blazer and gray flannel pants. "It's these clothes," he said. "They just don't like me. And they know the feeling's mutual."

"The clothes are fine," Cynthia said. "Very spiffy." She let her finger travel across a leaf labeled "Mr. and Mrs. Chris Goldenberg," then trailed it across their daughters Kate and Rebecca. "So what is it with you?" she asked. "Why are you standing here?"

Tuck shrugged. "Maybe a Dixie cup full of wine went to my head."

Around Cynthia's neck was a double strand of bright glass beads, which she raised to her mouth and nibbled at instead of answering him. "We married into the wrong family, you and I," she said at last.

He looked straight at her, startled. "What are you talking about?" he said. "You hardly even know me."

"It's not all that difficult, figuring out who a person is." She was back to her necklace again, scraping her front teeth against the frosted glass of a small, barrel-shaped bead.

"For so long," he said, "I wanted to win you over. It meant something to me."

Cynthia nodded her head slightly. "And now?"

"It's hard to say. Nothing seems so urgent anymore."

"I know," said Cynthia. "And let me tell you how good it feels to be out of the competition, finally. I look at Andrew and all I can think is: Why don't you go out and get yourself a haircut, buddy. That's what he inspires in me—not much. And it's a pleasure to have it come to that, let me tell you."

"What about me?" Tuck said.

"You?" said Cynthia. "Big mystery, but you're winning me over even as we speak."

Hearing this, he felt a little light-headed, as if he were suddenly unsure of his place in the world. He watched the people moving past them now in a steady flow, heading excitedly for the Burgundy Room, where the reception was about to begin. He grabbed Cynthia's hand and steered her down the hall, and they broke into laughter at precisely the same instant, because, after all, what could have been funnier than the thought of the two of them looking as if they were just another ordinary couple. The band was already playing music for a hora, and a noisy circle of about fifty people had formed on the dance floor. "They're playing our song," he shouted to Cynthia, and together they joined the circle, though Tuck had absolutely no idea of what was expected of him. He kicked up his feet along with everyone else and once or twice almost lost his balance as the circle turned faster and faster. In the center now were Brian and Andrew, beaming and spinning like madmen, while the dancers around them came to a halt and clapped rhythmically in tribute to them both. Someone tried to push Cynthia into the center. At first she resisted, laughing and apologizing and trying hard to stand firm, but a few more people ran over and seized her arms, thrusting her forward, and at last she gave in and joined Andrew and their son. The clapping went on, and everyone in the circle seemed to be smiling. Absently, Tuck clapped along, his palms stinging. He reminded himself that he wasn't a prisoner here, that he could walk away at any moment, out of the room, and the life he'd gone after so ardently. The time seemed right for taking leave of it all, but, for some reason he could not fathom, he simply let it pass.

The small circle within the larger one suddenly came apart, and the three dancers came tripping toward him now, their faces polished with exhilaration. It was Brian whose name he called out, Brian who was lifting his head toward Tuck to receive his kiss.

"You were wonderful," Tuck said, and meant it.

On line for the smorgasbord, sandwiched between Cynthia and Andrew, Tuck suffered a moment of panic, convinced that they would desert him now without warning, that he would end up sharing a meal with some ancient, half-deaf aunts and uncles, or, even worse, a tableful of young marrieds. But soon he reached the buffet table, and allowed his plate to be filled with pineapple chicken, kosher "spare ribs," and a mound of fried rice that was mostly bits of egg and green peas. He followed Andrew and Cynthia to an empty table and started on the chicken, though it looked unnaturally bright and gelatinous and was thoroughly unappealing.

"There's nothing more depressing than kosher Chinese food," Cynthia said cheerfully. "And I mean nothing."

"If you were footing the bill, you wouldn't be so quick to criticize," said Andrew.

"If I were footing the bill, we'd be sitting here with real food on our plates."

"My guess is that we'd be sharing six-foot-long hero sandwiches and drinking Bud Lite straight from the bottle."

"Look," said Cynthia, "I don't even want to be here. So the least you can do is let me know how terrific I look in my new mini skirt."

"Okay, stand up," said Andrew. "Nice legs," he offered, as Cynthia rose in a hurry and sat back down again, yanking her skirt down as far as it could go, which wasn't very far. "You always had nice legs," he murmured.

"I still don't want to be here," said Cynthia. "In fact, I'd rather be anywhere else."

"You keep saying that. So why did you come?"

"Because I'm a good mother and an exemplary ex-wife, that's why."

Without much interest, Tuck picked up a spare rib, which immediately slipped from his fingers and came to rest on the knee of his new gray pants before dropping to the floor.

"Seltzer," Cynthia advised. "It'll take out almost anything."

"Listen, Cindy," said Andrew, covering her wrist with his hand, "I'm spending thousands of dollars I can ill-afford for this shindig, so why can't you flatter me and tell me the food is great."

"Sorry," Cynthia said. "I just can't bring myself to—"

"The food is great," Tuck said. "Now can we please talk about something else?"

"No we can't," said Andrew fiercely. Rising from the table, he slid the food from his plate onto Cynthia's, and taking the empty plate along with him, stalked back to the buffet table.

Tuck and Cynthia smiled at each other briefly, unhappily, and then Tuck said, "You were really pretty hard on him, you know."

Cynthia nodded. "I hate this," she said. "I can't stay in the same room with these people. All during the ceremony, Andrew's mother kept reaching over him to squeeze my hand. I hate it that she feels she has to comfort me."

"But you want to be comforted," Tuck said. "Don't you?"

"All I want is to get out of here. Can you take me home?"

"Don't you have a car?"

"His parents insisted on picking me up," Cynthia said. "They say they want me to feel as if I'm still part of the family, which clearly I'm not. Do you understand what I'm telling you?" She caught sight of Brian then, who was rushing off with a pack of his friends across the floor. "Come here, you," she called out to him.

"Me?" he mouthed. He slung his arm around a tiny girl in high heels and grinned at his mother.

"I only need you for a minute," said Cynthia.

Brian whispered something in the girl's ear, making her laugh, and then he approached Cynthia. "What's up?" he said. His shoes were gone and his silk tie was entirely undone; when he leaned over to kiss her, the tie slid down one shoulder and fell into his mother's lap.

"You're such a beautiful boy," Cynthia said, wrapping the tie around her wrist. "Really."

"Is that all?" said Brian. "That's what you called me over here for?"

"That's it."

"Are you sure?"

"Go, sweetie," Cynthia said. "Have fun. I'll see you later." Turning to face Tuck, she said, "How about it? Will you take me home?"

"First I want to check on Andrew." When he found him, Andrew was sitting between his mother and father, looking distracted, drawing on the blue linen tablecloth with the tines of his fork. Tuck pulled gently on Andrew's ponytail. "Can I talk to you?"

"How about telling him I have a headache," Andrew instructed his mother.

"Can I offer you some Maximum Strength Anacin?" said Rosalind.

"I really need to talk to you, Andrew."

"I can't be reached right now," Andrew said gloomily. "Why don't you call back in a few hours."

"Or years," said Rosalind. "Whatever." She gave Tuck a long, curious look, the longest gaze he'd ever gotten from her. "There's a grease stain on your nice new pants," she said, and turned away from him. "You might try a little club soda," she said from over her shoulder a minute later. "And as a last resort, there's always hair spray."

"Shaving cream," said Andrew. "And that's my final word on this or any other subject, darling."

"Which darling is that?" said Tuck.

"You," said Rosalind. "It breaks my heart every time."

Cynthia lived a quick, fifteen-minute drive from the temple, but as soon as Tuck pulled up in front of her house, he understood that she had no immediate plans to leave the car. Flipping down the sun visor, she stared at herself in the mirror. She thrust her fingers through the loose curls of her permanent, until at last Tuck snapped the visor in place.

"I really ought to be getting back," he said.

"Why? Who's going to miss you?"

"You never know," said Tuck. He wanted to be there to savor the precise moment when Andrew would raise his head and begin to search the room for him, frantic with hope and desire, and full of regret. "Will you be all right alone?" he asked Cynthia.

"What do you think?"

Sighing, Tuck shut off the motor. "Let's talk," he said.

Cynthia stretched her arm in front of him and turned on the ignition. "We could go somewhere," she said.

"For a cup of coffee, you mean?"

"Take me on a tour of the store," Cynthia said. "I've never seen it, never even had a chance to press my nose against the glass."

"It's just a little gift shop," he said. "You know, dishes, silverware, nothing special."

Cynthia swiveled the button on the sleeve of his blazer. "Please," she said, not quite begging, but still making him feel as if he did not have the option of refusing her.

"You can't be serious," he said as he put the car in gear. He pressed forward on the accelerator and took off, curious to see where this would lead him.

He drove for under an hour, with Cynthia dozing all the way. Unlocking the door, he listened with pleasure to her sigh of astonishment when he ushered her inside. Watching her slow voyage through the room, her hands traveling across the surfaces of all the strange, lovely things within her reach, he saw what someone else, more generous, more knowing, might have seen with his eyes closed; that it was Andrew her hands were lingering over. He was lost to her, but here she was reclaiming him, dreamily rubbing a silk peach across her cheek, as if it were something beloved.

"You don't want him," Tuck said in a whispery voice, approaching her now and leading her away from the peach tree. "Not really." Holding on to her fingertips, he let her in on a few secrets—these days, Andrew was easily insulted, unforgiving, too often impatient. "This is a man who sprays air freshener in my face every time I light up a cigarette. Every time!" Tuck cried out, as if he could see the sweet-smelling mist trailing, like his lover's anger, in the air all around him. "Why would you want to share your life with a person like that?"

"You tell me," Cynthia said.

He did not answer her because there were, he knew, some secrets that simply could not be given away. And this is what he remembered: he and Andrew, overwhelmed by hilarity, sitting in their car, parked in the lot behind the store not too many weeks ago. There were tears of laughter in their eyes and they were slapping their hands against the dashboard. They had just returned from a shopping spree at the Salvation Army, where they'd bought a silk dress and accessories for their new mannequin, another five-foot-tall pig—a recent, unexplained gift from Andrew's old friend. "The saleswoman," Andrew wheezes, "the saleswoman says, 'So what size shoe does this alleged pig wear?'" And now, finally, they are stumbling inside, and Tuck is wiping the last tears from his eyes as Andrew sets to work on the pig. With great effort he eases her into a dress, first removing her head and handing it to Tuck, who holds it in his lap, then tosses it around like a basketball. Ignoring him, Andrew ties a rope of fake pearls around the pig's waist, and then retrieves the head, upon which he rests a floppy white hat. In one hand he places a lace handkerchief, in the other, a delicate-looking wineglass. He seats the pig at a table set for four, crosses her legs at the knee, and arranges one spiked heel on her foot so that it dangles, perfectly balanced, from her toes. "Like magic," Tuck breathes, and touches the slow measure of contentment that falls soundlessly across Andrew's face.

"Oh, Cynthia," he said now, pressing her head gently against him and stroking her soft hair, but falling in love all over again, he had already forgotten her.

Ice

~~~~~~~~~~
~~~~~~~~~~

Daisy has known for a long time that Vivian has flipped, is losing her marbles one by one. It's been a painful thing to witness and sometimes Daisy cries over it, but discreetly, so that Vivian won't notice and say, "*Now* what are you crying about?" Vivian is her live-in companion, and her salary is paid by Daisy's sister, who had the good sense to marry a rich man and hang on to him forever. Daisy's husband sold apples on street corners during the depression and was never quite the same after that, never quite able to recover from the loss of dignity. He lived uneasily for another twenty-five years and then he fell sick and died, without giving much advance warning.

"Cancerous," Daisy says out loud, but Vivian ignores her and goes on with what she's doing, which is hurling handfuls of ice cubes from a five-pound plastic bag to the living room floor, then smashing the ice with the bottoms of her thick-soled walking shoes. This is to exorcise the smell of evil that Vivian claims has permeated the apartment. According to Vivian, ice cubes are the only thing that will do the trick. That and the ammonia she has poured all over the lovely parquet flooring. Watching her, Daisy says, "The landlord's going to have our heads, yours and mine both, I guarantee it."

"The evil," says Vivian, "is everywhere in this apartment."

"Don't you know what all this ammonia is doing to you?" Daisy says. "It's destroying your lungs, that's what." She picks herself up from the couch and wanders into the kitchen, where she fixes two bowls of Frosted Mini-Wheats and milk, and adds some sliced banana. She is a small woman with surprisingly long, beautiful legs. Her hair is thick and white, cut short with bangs, like a young girl. ("A pixie cut," Daisy calls it.) She spent most of her life as a bookkeeper and was furious when, long ago, she reached seventy and was forced to give up her job. ("A clear case of anti-Semitism," she insists.)

"This is the Lord's work I'm doing," Vivian hollers. "So don't give me any lectures about lung tissue."

"Are you too busy doing the Lord's work to have some dinner?" Daisy asks. No response. She flicks on the radio next to her cereal bowl and listens to a call-in show that is hosted by a psychologist. She loves listening to this show, which makes her feel as if she is right out there in the middle of the world, missing nothing. The caller speaking now is a woman with three grown children, two sons and a daughter. Her sons, the woman says in a trembly voice, are homosexuals, her daughter a lesbian. "It's a pitiful thing," Daisy says. The woman begins to weep as she talks about her children. The psychologist, also a woman, advises the caller that tears are sometimes productive. "Go ahead and cry," the psychologist urges. The woman weeps on the radio for a moment or two longer, and soon there is a click: She has hung up. Daisy is crying, too. She thinks of calling the psychologist and saying, "My friend is losing her marbles." Of course, she'd make an effort to put it a little more delicately: "My friend is so busy doing the Lord's work that she forgets about eating and sleeping and doing the grocery shopping. Not to mention the laundry." Daisy looks down at her housecoat. It's a paisley pattern against a dark background and doesn't show much dirt. She brings a sleeve up close to her face and sniffs the fabric. "Vivian," she yells. "If cleanliness is next to godliness, I'd advise you to hop to it and get a laundry together."

Vivian appears in the kitchen, tracking slivers of ice onto the linoleum. She is dressed in a short white uniform, white stockings with runs leading straight up from her knees, and white oxfords. Above her breast pocket is a plastic name badge that says "Vivienne." For years she worked at New York Hospital as a nurse's aide, until one day she felt too old and cranky for the job and decided to quit. (Or else it was the patients who were too old and cranky; Daisy could never remember which.) Vivian has four children, all boys, who send her flowers on Mother's Day—hearts and horseshoes covered with carnations, and once, a single white lily that Vivian dumped immediately into the trash. ("The flower of death," she hissed, as Daisy went right into the garbage and retrieved the lily, saying, "Even the flower of death has got to be better than no flowers at all on Mother's Day.") The rest of the year, Vivian doesn't hear a peep from any of them. "Once they've grown, you can forget it," she tells Daisy. "Children need you like a hole in the head and that's okay. Anyway, what can you do with four big tall men who get tangled up in your furniture and mess up your house with no regard for how much effort it takes to keep things in order?" Daisy understands. Her daughter, Elizabeth, has lived in Los Angeles for several years now. She complains on the phone every week that it's a city full of shallow people but at least the weather is good. "Catch a plane and come visit," Elizabeth always says. "My treat. And, of course, bring Vivian with you." Daisy and Vivian find this hilarious. Neither of them has ever been on a plane and they have no interest in risking their necks for a little good weather. Whenever she thinks about it, Daisy has to admit that she enjoyed Elizabeth more as a child: all that kissing and hugging and open declarations of love. Still, she wishes she weren't afraid to travel across the sky like the rest of the world. On bad days, she misses Elizabeth with an ache that settles under her skin and will not budge, like Vivian when she mopes in the Barcalounger, contemplating the evil she's convinced is thriving right under her nose. ("Why here?" Daisy wants to know. "What's so special about this broken-down rat trap, anyway?" But Vivian's not giving any answers.)

Vivian sinks down into a seat at the table and takes Daisy's face into her hands. "Oh, Jesus," she says, squinting at her. "Jeepers."

"Eat your cereal," says Daisy. "Notice that there's some banana in there, plenty of potassium for you." Vivian is smaller than Daisy and thin, growing thinner all the time, it seems. Daisy worries that one day she'll slip right out of her uniform and just disappear, leaving behind only a puddle of white.

"You've got whiskers growing out of your chin," Vivian announces. "Just like a man." Her fingers against Daisy's face smell strongly of ammonia; Daisy pushes them away.

"Hormones," says Daisy. "Too little of one kind, too much of the other." She tries to make light of it, but brushing her fingertips over her chin, she feels herself blushing.

"Don't you move from that table, miss," Vivian says. Soon Daisy hears her making noise in the bathroom, fooling around in the medicine cabinet. Bottles of pills tumble into the sink; something made of metal clatters to the tiled floor.

"Easy," Daisy yells. "One of these days you're going to destroy this place altogether. Raze it right to the ground."

Then Vivian is standing over her with a pair of manicure scissors and a small bottle of Mercurochrome. Daisy shoves the back of her chair against the wall, covers her face with one arm. "Not today, thanks," she says.

Smiling, Vivian says, "We've been together for what, three, four years now, and all of a sudden you're backing away from me?"

"Seven," says Daisy.

"Imagine that," says Vivian. "I must have lost track of the time somehow." Slowly she lowers Daisy's arm from her face, squeezes her hand in a friendly way.

"Somehow," says Daisy, shutting her eyes as Vivian comes toward her with the manicure scissors. Then she tells Vivian, "You remind me of my mother-in-law. She didn't care much for me and I didn't care much for her, and one day she sneaks up behind me and cuts off a piece of my hair just for spite."

"A deranged woman," says Vivian. She snips cautiously at Daisy's chin. "My poor baby doll," she says. She dots Daisy's chin with Mercurochrome, to prevent infection, she says.

"How about a mirror?" says Daisy, and immediately changes her mind "Not a pretty picture, I'm sure," she says.

"Don't be so hard on yourself. You're cute as a button," says Vivian. "For an old lady."

"Old old old," Daisy says, tapping a spoon on the edge of her glass cereal bowl. "What's the point?" Rising and walking to the kitchen window, she rests against the blistered ledge and stares two stories down to the street corner. Lights have just been turned on in the dusk below. It is nearly April now, nearly spring. She watches as some teenagers strip a long black car parked in front of the apartment house: first the hubcaps, front and rear, then the antenna. A radio and two small speaker boxes are next. The thieves are thin boys in their shirtsleeves. Daisy raises the window. "Why do you work so hard to make your parents ashamed of you?" she hollers to them. "How about a Blaupunkt radio, cheap?" one of the boys yells back. Daisy goes to the phone, dials 911, and is put on hold. Eventually, a woman comes on and takes down the information. She is bored with the details, bored with Daisy. At the end of the conversation she says, "Have a nice day."

"This neighborhood," Daisy says, rubbing her chin with two fingers. When she takes her hand away, her fingers are bright orange with Mercurochrome.

Vivian lights a cigarette and tosses the match into one of the cereal bowls, where it sizzles for an instant, then floats between two slices of banana. She smokes without speaking, leaning one elbow on the table, her head propped against her palm. "There's nothing wrong with this neighborhood that a few bombs couldn't cure," she says finally.

Nodding, Daisy says, "I'm going to watch my boyfriends, Mr. MacNeil and Mr. Lehrer, on the television."

"Boyfriends!" Vivian hoots. "Any minute there's going to be a knock on the door, right, and the delivery boy will be saying, 'Flowers from MacNeil/Lehrer!' right?" She laughs in that choked way that Daisy doesn't like, soundlessly, her feet stamping hard under the table.

"Well, at this point, they're the only boyfriends I've got," Daisy says, but she has to laugh at the thought of those flowers arriving and the miniature card tucked inside the miniature envelope that says, "To our sweetie pie."

"Got any money?" Vivian asks when at last she stops laughing.

"You finally decide to do the grocery shopping?"

"Just going out for ice," says Vivian, and Daisy is amazed at how ordinary and innocent the words sound, as if she had said, "Just going out for a pack of cigarettes." It's the ordinary sound of it that gives Daisy a chill, along with Vivian's round eyes, wide-open with alarm.

"What do you see?" Daisy asks for the hundredth time. Not that she expects to get an answer. On the subject of "the evil" (as Daisy thinks of it), Vivian is resolutely inarticulate.

Abruptly, Vivian shrugs her shoulders and says, "Can I have two dollars?"

Daisy breathes through her teeth. The shrug makes her feel desolate, as if Vivian were already far away, striding down the block toward the supermarket, a tiny dark madwoman with the moon shining on the shoulders of her hooded corduroy coat.

Vivian is holding out her hand, palm upward. "Ten dollars, please," she says patiently.

"Beggar," says Daisy, but not loud enough for Vivian to hear. She tears off the month of February from a small calendar perched on top of a low glass-and-wood cabinet. On the back she makes a list: 99% fat free (one qt.), cottage cheese (California style), Hydrox cookies, toothpaste (anything but Crest). "This is an act of faith, Vivian," she says, handing her the list and a ten-dollar bill.

"That February was something else," Vivian says. "I must have had to use about thirty pounds of ice, maybe more." Out into the dark hallway she goes, hood up around her face, a large pair of men's canvas work gloves covering her hands.

In the living room, Daisy turns on the TV, but the tenant in the apartment directly overhead has decided to vacuum. Daisy gets a broom and bangs bravely on the ceiling; all she gets is more static. She shuts off the set and calls her sister Elsie on Sutton Place.

"Oh," says Elsie, "hello and goodbye. You caught me in the middle of a Great Books night. A few of my lady friends are over and we're doing Dante's *Inferno.*"

"The *Inferno?*" says Daisy, and laughs. "You ought to invite Vivian to join your group. That's right up her alley these days."

"Vivian?"

"I'm worried sick, to tell you the truth."

"Is it money?" Elsie whispers into the phone. "I can write you a check in the morning."

"She's ruining my living room floor," says Daisy, "but that's the least of it."

"Do you need wall-to-wall carpeting?" says Elsie. "I'd be glad to send somebody over from Macy's—"

"It isn't that," Daisy tells her. "It's something unearthly, I think."

"I have to hang up now," her sister says. "You can let me know about the carpeting later."

Sitting in the Barcalounger, her feet tilted toward the ceiling, hands folded into fists in her lap, Daisy says, "Damn." She remembers the years of her life that were spent at an adding machine, getting things right, making sense of things. Tiresome work, though she has to admit she was good at it. But what does she know of unearthly things? She doesn't have much patience left. Ice storms in her living room, shards of melting ice everywhere; the sharp, unpleasant scent of ammonia lingering on her skin, her clothes. But in all the world there is only Vivian calling her *baby doll,* cupping her face in her hands, painting her delicately with Mercurochrome. At the end of your life, you're no fool; you take what is offered.

Later, past midnight, long after Vivian has come back with her bags of ice, Daisy dreams of a carpet of shattered glass spread shimmering over the floor. In her warm bed she shivers, and slides deep under the covers.

Leaving Johanna

~~~~~~~~~~~~~~~~~~~~~~~~~~~~~

He's made up his mind that he will leave her, knowing that he can never tell her the real reasons, which are painful and complicated and certain to hurt her deeply. A simple, unimaginative lie will make things easier on them both: He will tell her he has fallen in love with someone else. It happens all the time—all over the world, at any given moment, people are falling swiftly and recklessly in love. She will be hurt—he can see the luminous tears in her dark, round eyes—but she will get over it before too long. (He met someone else, she'll tell her mother and probably a friend or two, and each of them will have at least one story for her that will prove that people have been there before, that there is nothing extraordinary about what has happened to her.)

They have been together for eight years, seven of them in New York City, where they are living now. Before that, Charles and Johanna were students in Ann Arbor, sharing the bottom floor of a run-down Victorian house with four cats named John, Paul, George, and Ringo. Their apartment in New York is in a limestone town house, a bright, high-ceilinged apartment with white wicker furniture and a huge white bookcase covering a whole wall of the living room. They are a block and a half from the park, where they ride their bicycles every Sunday, weather permitting. Their life together has been a quiet one—mostly they have been content to be alone together. They have never married, for reasons that sound, Charles realizes, a little lame; they both come from divorced families and simply do not see marriage as necessary or desirable.

Johanna is barely five feet tall and is thin everywhere, like a child who needs several more summers to fill out. Charles has never seen her eat a full meal. Half a sandwich or a plate of salad is enough for her. Whenever they go out to restaurants, they often end up sharing a single meal, and he is always hungry afterward. He will go home and fix some food for himself, and Johanna will sit with him and watch him eat, claiming to be so stuffed she can hardly move. He can't believe anyone could be satisfied with so little.

Every morning, before he leaves for work, he makes lunch for her, the same lunch every day, patiently adding Havarti and roast beef and alfalfa sprouts to pita bread, wrapping it neatly in aluminum foil, along with what looks like the quintessential apple or orange, which he spent a long time choosing from a fruit stand the night before. He will slip the package into the canvas bag she carries to work, and threaten her with an unspeakable fate if she doesn't eat it. How was your lunch, he asks her at dinnertime. Did you eat any of it? She enjoys teasing him and will say that she traded it for some magic beans or sold it on the black market. He tells himself that of course she ate it, or at least most of it, because it's too depressing to think of her dumping his carefully made lunch into the garbage, day after day.

After eight years, Charles often finds himself day-dreaming about other women he knows; calm, soft-looking women who strike him as instinctively generous, who seem to enjoy being of comfort to anyone who wants it of them. It's this tender, sheltering presence he's tired of doing without, he has come to realize—the kind of lover who will occasionally reach for him as if he is someone in need. He's tired of feeling protective, responsible, always watchful; of feeling that he is, more than anything else, Johanna's guardian. And the things he once thought endearing—her childlike size and appearance, her dependence on him for so many small things, all the ways she needs to be taken care of—have begun to seem like failures on her part. He wonders if he has just opened his eyes to a reality that everyone who knows her had recognized long ago.

Over and over again, Charles tries to persuade himself that Johanna, without him, will manage perfectly well. Like everyone else, she will prepare meals, pay the bills, balance the checkbook. She is certainly capable of performing all these tasks, despite the fact that she has somehow managed to convince them both that almost everything is too much for her, that they are better off if he is in charge. He once overheard her confiding to a friend that she was too fragile, too uneasy about too many things to keep her life running smoothly by herself. It was the word *fragile* that made Charles flinch, as if he were drawing back from something instantly and unexpectedly painful.

• • •

On his way home from work, on the subway, Charles looks up from his newspaper and sees a woman he recognizes standing alone, her hands gripping the metal pole in front of her for balance. The woman has beautiful pale blond hair that she wears in braids that are pinned up and crossed at the back of her head. The last time he saw her, when they were standing next to each other in a subway car several months ago, her hair was pulled tight in a high ponytail that had brushed against his face when she turned her head. She is as tall as he, and very sunburned, though it is midwinter. There is an attaché case between her feet; every now and then she glances down to make sure it's still there.

He offers her his seat, though there is an elderly man close by who gives him a dirty look that Charles pretends not to see. This is a mistake; as the blond woman slips into the seat, the old man glares and asks her, loudly, where she was brought up.

"Connecticut," the woman says, looking confused.

"Oh, so they have barnyards there, too," the old man says. Charles would like to kill him.

The blond woman is on her feet, making her way quickly across the floor into the next car. Charles considers running after her, but then the train jerks to a stop between stations, the lights flicker and die, and there's no longer a decision to be made.

Johanna is frying ground beef in a large blackened pan, adding spices like crazy—pepper, chili powder, garlic salt, dry mustard. Still in his overcoat, Charles comes up behind her and takes the tin of mustard from her hand. "Careful," he says.

"Hi, sweetie. I didn't hear you come in," she says, then turns around to kiss him. She is dressed in white painters' pants and a red turtleneck, and over that, one of his oxford shirts with the sleeves rolled up. The shirt is so big on her it looks ridiculous, clownish, as if she were a kid dressing up, parading around in her father's clothes. He is surprised to see her making dinner, surprised at how cheerful and energetic she seems. On a chopping block next to the stove, he sees small orderly piles of diced tomato, olives, cheese, and shredded lettuce. Apparently she's been busy in the kitchen for some time.

He asks how her day went.

"As a matter of fact," she says, stirring the meat with a long-handled wooden spoon, "I quit my job and I feel pretty good about it, sort of exhilarated, actually."

He sucks in his breath, then breathes out slowly. "We never talked about this," he says. "Am I right that I'm hearing this for the first time?"

"I was never going to get promoted, Charles. There was nowhere for me to go. I was just spinning my wheels." She smiles at him. "You look so worried. Give me a month or so and I'll have it all worked out."

"Johanna," he says. His coat is still on. He doesn't want to give her a month, or even a week. He's all set to make his move, but he has no courage. What is he afraid of? She's twenty-nine years old, old enough for anything. His leaving may even turn out to be just what she needs —an ideal opportunity to find out exactly what she can do for herself. He suspects, though, that this is a long way from the truth.

He has no appetite at all, and eats only with great effort. Johanna has four tacos to his two. He's never seen her eat so much, and he worries that something is wrong. "Will you still love me if I blow up like a blimp?" Johanna asks laughingly.

At the end of the meal they do the dishes together, with the stereo in the far corner of the living room turned up so high he can barely hear himself think.

• • •

Later, walking down Columbus Avenue in search of ice cream, Johanna slips her arm around his waist. "I can't wait for summer," she says. "I'm so sick of trying to keep warm all the time." She huddles against him, though it's a windless, comfortable night—too warm for the gloves and scarf he has on, Charles realizes. He takes them off and stuffs them into the pockets of his jacket.

"You're sure you want ice cream?" he asks.

"Sure."

Glassed-in cafés on both sides of the street are filled with customers, the street itself almost as crowded as if it were spring. Waiting for their money to emerge from a Citibank cash machine, two men pass a joint back and forth, giggling softly. One of the men is extremely handsome, the other ordinary-looking. Both are obviously gay. A black man dressed in fluorescent yellow pants roller-skates gracefully in the bicycle lane, jumping and twisting in the air. As Charles and Johanna cross the street, a young boy, no older than twelve or thirteen, stretches out his arm and thrusts a leaflet at Charles. "Check it out, get laid," he says cheerfully. He's wearing big white plastic sunglasses and a three-piece suit, and is smoking a cigarette. Charles sighs and throws away the leaflet without reading it. He is thinking that it will be hard for Johanna to find someone suitable. According to the women in his office, the situation is just about impossible. Everyone is either married or gay, they complain. His own assistant has been involved with a married man for years. He and his wife had just had a baby with Down's syndrome, she told Charles, weeping in his office one day a few weeks ago. At first Charles thought she was weeping out of sympathy for her lover, but then he suspected it was only because she knew that now the man would never leave his wife. Never, she said, kicking the side of his desk with the toe of her boot. Not under those circumstances.

"Here we go," Johanna says, leading him into the Ice

Cream Boutique, a long, narrow store where he orders a single scoop of Swiss chocolate almond for the two of them to share. There's nowhere to sit, except for a bench of varnished blond wood that's nailed to the sidewalk opposite the store. Charles wants to keep walking, but Johanna says she'd like to sit down for a minute.

"Tired?" he asks her.

She shakes her head and takes the cone from him. "Just in the mood to sit a while." A teenage girl in an extraordinarily short black skirt, black tights, and black, ankle-high boots pushes a child in a fancy-looking stroller into the ice-cream store. The child has a slice of pizza in his lap; tomato sauce brightens his lips. "I hope to God she's the baby-sitter and not the mother," Johanna says, sounding gloomy.

Charles is silent. "Johanna," he says finally, when the girl comes out with her ice-cream cone. He stares at the girl, watches her walk down the street with the stroller. "Listen to me," he says. He tells her that he is in love, that he has a lover who means everything to him. His voice fades in and out, as if the words were coming from a great distance, along miles of telephone line. Then, because he can't help feeling ashamed, he starts to apologize. The apology seems to go on forever; there's no end to it, no end to the clichéd bits of optimism that come effortlessly to mind.

"I don't believe you," Johanna says slowly.

"What?" His face radiates heat; his mouth is unbearably dry. He reaches for the ice-cream cone, but then holds it in his hand without eating it.

"I don't believe that after eight years you could actually let something like this happen."

"I know," Charles says. His head droops. Ice cream slides between his fingers, down his hand, and underneath the cuff of his jacket sleeve.

"How long have you known her?"

"Not too long," Charles says. "A couple of months, maybe."

"What's her name?"

"Arden," he says. He's startled by the question, even more startled by the swiftness of his answer.

Johanna looks puzzled. "What kind of name is that?"

"You don't like it?" he says. It's the name of a little girl who was walking in front of him with her mother on Fifth Avenue this afternoon—a child whose mother kept saying to her, "You'll get nothing if you keep this up. Absolutely nothing. Just remember that."

"Charles," Johanna says, her voice slightly raised, "what's the matter with you? You tell me your lover's name, and then you're worried I won't like it? If I told you I didn't like it, would you change it to something that sounded better?"

"I'm sorry," Charles says. "I seem to be having a little trouble."

"You have ice cream all over your jacket."

"I know."

Johanna sighs, looks at him with exasperation but also pity, he thinks. She gets up from her seat, goes into the Boutique, and returns with a handful of napkins and a large paper cup of water. She wets one of the napkins and rubs at the stains on his jacket. "I might as well tell you, I've always thought we were made for each other," she says. "I've thought that from day one. Of course, if only one of us believes it, I must be mistaken."

There is nothing he can say, nothing that seems appropriate. He slides his hand into the cup of water, spattering drops on the tips of Johanna's shoes, but she doesn't seem to notice. She is slowly opening and closing her hands, staring at the movement of her fingers. "Arden," she says. She says the name over and over again, whispering it like a secret.

• • •

In the morning, as Charles is dressing for work, Johanna insists that he answer a few more questions. She sits in the middle of their bed in a white flannel nightgown, her arms wrapped around her legs, her chin resting against her knees. He owes her that much, she says. Just a few answers to a few simple questions. What does Arden look like, she wants to know. He closes his eyes, sees the blond woman on the subway. Tall, he says. Thick blond hair. Pretty? Pretty hair, he says. Johanna nods. What kind of job does she have? He remembers the woman's expensive-looking attaché case, Mark Cross, maybe. She works for IBM, he says. Some kind of management position. Does she have an M.B.A.? Easy question: yes or no. He starts to relax a little. Stanford Business School, better than Harvard, he says. Johanna frowns at this, saying, She must be pretty bright. He doesn't contradict her. He says he is going to be late for work, and doesn't have time to sit here answering a thousand questions. But he doesn't mean it the way it sounds. He touches her arm. Forgive me, he says. He's not himself today.

One last question, Johanna says, shaking off his hand. Is she married? Divorced, he tells her. Six years of marriage, one child, a little girl named Whitney Rose. Answers flow from some mysterious source; he's like a fortune-teller who knows he's a fraud, and can't listen to the sound of his voice without being amazed by it.

It figures, Johanna says, laughing out loud. It figures that a woman with a name like that would go and name her kid Whitney Rose.

He's sweating through his shirt; two large crescent-shaped stains feel cold against his ribs. And he feels awful, exhausted and weak. He slept badly last night, keeping all the way to one side of the bed, fearful of his foot accidentally grazing Johanna's ankle, or his arm coming to rest across her stomach. He had offered to sleep on the living room couch and was surprised when Johanna told him it wasn't necessary. We're not enemies, she said coolly. Just think of us as two well-acquainted people sharing a mattress and some blankets. He understood then that she was calling the shots, that he would not be the one to deny her anything. He was the one who had set things in motion, who had harmed her, earning her contempt. Incredibly, she made him feel as if the losses were all his, as if she were the one who had suddenly withdrawn her love, support, friendship, everything.

He sips at a small Oriental soup bowl filled with herbal tea while Johanna sits across from him at the kitchen table reading a magazine.

"I forgot to make your lunch," he says. "Promise me you'll eat something today."

"I promise you nothing," she says without looking up from the magazine.

"You'll get sick," Charles says.

"Just remember who you are," Johanna says. She closes the magazine and slaps it against the tabletop. "You're merely an ex-lover, with no rights or privileges whatsoever."

"You don't have to be that way," he says.

"Oh, I get it," Johanna says. "You and Arden are supposed to simply fade into the sunset, after I've given you a kiss good-bye and wished you well."

Arden. It chills him to think that to Johanna she is flesh and bone, the very real object of her anger and pain. Johanna is probably dying to track her down, to study her until she's memorized her feature by feature. Inappropriately, he smiles, then clamps a fist over his mouth.

"You're out to lunch, kiddo," Johanna says. "If I were you, I'd be scared to death."

"Of what?"

"I see people like you on the street all the time. They're well-dressed, look perfectly normal, and then all of a sudden you notice that their lips are moving, that they're talking to themselves a mile a minute. They're space cadets masquerading as regular people." Johanna goes back to her magazine. "Have a good day at work," she says.

Franny, his assistant, is sitting at her desk crying. She puts her hand up in greeting as Charles walks by. "Don't pay any attention to me," she says. "Just pretend these are tears of joy."

He gestures toward his office, waits for her to gather tissues, cigarettes, and a lighter together. In his office she settles into a swivel chair and turns from side to side, saying nothing. The chair squeaks at every other turn.

"Tom's baby has to have heart surgery," Franny says finally, sitting still now. "He's sick over it. He came to my apartment last night and pretty much fell apart. The two of us drank too much and cried for hours."

Charles sits behind his desk and sifts paper clips through his fingers. "Why do you keep on seeing him? What do you get out of it?" he says softly.

Smiling at him, Franny says, "Every six months or so, we split up. I usually quit smoking then, too, and go on a diet, all in preparation for my new, improved life. Ten days later we're back together again, I'm buying cigarettes by the carton, and eating like a horse."

"So," Charles says, "you don't really want a new, improved life after all."

Franny begins to cry again. "What kind of person am I? The three nights his wife was in the hospital after she'd had the baby, he stayed over at my apartment. I didn't invite him, he invited himself, but the point is that I let him stay."

"He needed you," Charles says.

"He thinks the baby is his punishment for not loving his wife enough, for hanging around with me all these years."

"Things happen. There doesn't always have to be a reason."

"He's making *me* feel guilty, too," Franny says. "It's as if he were holding me partly responsible."

Charles gets up and walks over to where she is sitting, squats down on the carpet, and rests his hands on the chrome arms of her chair. "You can't really believe that," he says.

Franny shakes her head, unable to talk. He has never seen anyone cry so hard. There is pale blue eye shadow smudged at the sides of her face. Blue eye shadow with tiny flecks of glitter. He sees her sitting at her makeup mirror this morning, a large oval mirror bordered by bright bulbs. She puts on her makeup as carefully as she types his letters, which are nearly always perfect. Now her cheeks are blue and glittery, not what she intended at all. He takes a tissue from her hand and wipes away the color, imagining, crazily, that this is Johanna, her face tear-soaked, absolutely inconsolable.

Arriving home in the early evening, Charles walks through the door into his apartment, then stops dead under the rounded archway that leads to the living room. He has to reach out for something to hold on to—the top of a ceramic umbrella stand is what he grabs first. Hanging from the light fixture in the middle of the ceiling, a noose around its neck, is a large stuffed animal, a panda that he'd bought for Johanna when they were in college. Charles puts a hand across his chest, waits for his heart to stop thumping. Then he goes into the bedroom to find Johanna, who is on the floor, still dressed in her nightgown, putting nail polish on her toenails. Grieg's Piano Concerto is on the radio, the volume a little too loud.

"I almost had a heart attack out there," Charles says. "Are you listening to me?"

Johanna raises an arm in the air, then lets it fall across the top of her head. "It was an awful thing to do, I know. But I had this desperate urge to do something destructive, and that was the best I could come up with."

"So what else did you do today, besides playing hangman?"

"Do you really care?"

"You're still in your nightgown," Charles says. "It worries me."

"Listen, I feel terrible that I frightened you, Charles. You probably think I'm insane."

"Forget it." Charles goes to his closet and changes into jeans and a sweater. "Did you eat today?"

"I listened to a lot of music and stared at the four walls."

"I'll take you out to dinner," he offers. "Dinner and a genuine effort to provide an evening of lighthearted chatter."

"Do you know anyone with a light heart?"

"Not personally," Charles says. "Do you?"

"What about Arden?" Johanna leans over and blows on her polished nails. "What could be bothering her?"

"I have a suggestion," Charles says. "You don't mention her tonight and I won't tell anyone that you hung me in effigy today."

"Actually, I've been thinking about her a lot. Are you going to move in with her?"

"I'm not sure what's going to happen."

"Maybe she's having second thoughts," Johanna says. "Now that you're free and available, maybe she's not so sure she wants you."

"That's enough," Charles says. "I'm dead serious."

"She loves you, but not quite as wholeheartedly as you'd like her to."

"I'll just close my eyes and listen to the music," Charles says. "Say anything you like."

Johanna walks awkwardly on her heels to the radio and shuts it off. "It's Whitney Rose, isn't it? She's afraid the kid may not like having you around all the time. She wants to ease you into the family gradually, so it won't be such a traumatic experience for the kid."

"We have to talk about the checking account," Charles says. "There are business matters that we have to take care of."

"Eight years," Johanna says, and drops slowly to the floor on her knees. "After a while, it's entirely possible to forget what it's like to be alone."

He thinks of the times they've been apart over the years, mostly visiting family. He always felt slightly uneasy without her, traveling by himself with only a book or two for company. They called each other from wherever they were—long-distance calls that transformed their voices into hollow-sounding versions of their true selves. You sound so strange, he'd tell her. I can't quite picture you. Tell me what you're wearing so I can see you. She always had to describe her clothes precisely, even her jewelry, and they always laughed afterward, imagining what strangers would think if they heard her end of the conversation. Once, when his father had cancer surgery and Charles went out to Cleveland for a week, he ended up daydreaming about Johanna constantly, but the images were hazy, as if she were a stranger who had never been within his reach, someone he could only fantasize about. Coming home to her at the end of the week, he was so overwhelmed by the sight of her, he nearly knocked her over at the airport gate. He must have been crazy in love with her then, though he can barely remember the feel of it; the urgency that defined their love.

"Please don't talk to me," Johanna says.

"What?"

"You look pained, and I can't bear to hear it right now."

"Just a little nostalgia," Charles says. "And some confusion, I guess." He rubs at his eyes, sighs quietly. "What about dinner?"

"Actually, I've made other plans," Johanna says. She pauses; he understands that she's trying to decide whether or not to tell the truth. "I'm going to my mother's tonight."

"That's all right." Oddly, he feels let down, as if having dinner with her were something he had been looking forward to all day.

For the next two weeks, at least, he's found a comfortable place to stay—Franny's L-shaped studio on the East Side, off First Avenue in a small sand-colored building whose hallways are poorly lit and smell like his mother's pot roast. Franny has escaped to San Francisco, leaving him to water the two huge rubber plants that stand in metal tubs at either side of her pull-out couch and to watch over her Himalayan cat, whose name he's already forgotten. He didn't explain to Franny why he was so eager to house-sit for her, but there was gratitude on all sides, and that was all that really mattered. He left Johanna his phone number and address on a large piece of paper that he watched her fold carefully into a tiny square and slip into her pants pocket without comment. And when he bent over and dropped an awkward kiss on the top of her head, she kept her back toward him. Hands at her elbows, he turned her around slowly. Out of nowhere tears came to his eyes the moment he saw her face, which was bleached and frightened-looking, easy to read. "It's like diving into ice water," she said quietly. "Nothing can prepare you for it, for the way it's going to feel."

After three days, he got over the urge to search through Franny's drawers for secrets—a locked diary, perhaps, letters from her lover, from her mother and father begging her to wise up and start looking for someone suitable, a man who can give her the things she really needs. The apartment is neat, and also very clean, except for the cream-colored balls of cat fur he finds against the baseboards and under the table. There are no bookcases in the apartment, just a three-tiered étagère filled with glass animals—lots of cats in different positions, a seal, a swan, a frog on a lily pad. The few books Franny owns are cookbooks for someone on a diet and one stained paperback entitled *The Junk Food Junkie's Book of Haute Cuisine;* they're lined up on top of the refrigerator, their covers coated lightly with grease. Her kitchen cabinets, at least, he can go through without feeling guilty; he's approached them each time with some excitement, as if he were doing something dishonorable after all. He opens one he hasn't touched before, and finds a canister filled with small pink envelopes of Sweet 'N Low, probably taken from restaurant tables (he smiles at this—his mother has been doing the same thing for years), rows of Campbell's soups, every one of them cream of mushroom, and way in the back, a partially filled-out application form from a computer dating service. The questionnaire asks what Franny believes in: natural foods, fate, witchcraft, a Supreme Being, or women's lib. Franny had checked off "fate," then crossed it out and checked "none of the above."

He turns away from the cabinets as the cat walks into the kitchen, weaving her way between Charles's ankles, meowing sharply. "I feel bad not knowing your name, kiddo," Charles says. "I do, however, remember what you like to do in your spare time." He tears a small sheet of aluminum foil from a roll sitting on the counter, crumples it into a shiny ball, then tosses it over his head toward the windows at the back of the apartment. The cat shoots after it, picks up the foil in her mouth, and drops it at Charles's feet. She looks up at him, then stands on her hind legs and puts her front paws against his knees. Her eyes are a very light blue, like Franny's. "Care to dance?" Charles asks, bending to take her paws in his hands. Her face smells like leather, like the inside of Franny's shoe where she's been resting her head all evening.

The phone rings for the first time in three days; he rushes to answer it. It's a wrong number, and he finds himself patiently explaining this to the high-pitched voice on the other end asking for one order of pork fried rice, one order of sliced chicken Hunan style, and one order of Buddha's Delight. The phone rings again almost as soon as he's hung up. "And no MSG," the voice says. This time there are other voices in the background, and the muffled laughter of teenage girls.

"Thanks for calling," Charles says, laughing. He waits for the girl to call back, but she doesn't. The idea, obviously, was for him to get furious, to slam down the phone in a rage. It has always taken a lot to get him angry, he thinks. He and Johanna rarely fought. Whenever they had an argument, he eventually turned his back on her, walking away before she could finish what she had to say. It was simple, really; so much easier than trading insults back and forth—contests he almost always lost through lack of enthusiasm. In the long run, he felt, there was very little worth fighting over. It used to drive Johanna wild the way he would walk out of a room or clamp headphones over his ears and lose himself in music so hard and loud it would pulse in his chest like a heartbeat. Once, she had pulled the headphones from his ears and thrown them to the floor. You have to talk to me, she screamed. You have to answer me. He had picked up the headphones and hung them around his neck, straining to hear the music from them as he calmed Johanna, whose anger, he remembers now, had been sparked by the way he'd gone on touching her long after she'd complained that his hands were cold.

He was always bewildered at the way small things would get to her—a look that flickered across a friend's face while Johanna was talking to her, a tone of voice that struck her as slightly impatient, the half-moment of hesitancy before her mother agreed to do something for her. You're not tuned in to subtleties, Johanna would tell him. Maybe not, but he was sure he was all the better for it. That had to be the reason she was so emotionally drained half the time—Johanna was too caught up in subtleties. She is probably playing him over and over in her mind, like a reel of film, the way he moved and sounded the night he so clumsily cut himself off from her, deliberately set himself adrift. And it's true, he realizes, that he is now without mooring. He has been held in place by love for so long that he is afraid of losing his balance without it.

His back straight, his arms swinging, looking, he imagines, like someone who knows exactly where he's headed and exactly what he wants, he goes to the phone and calls Johanna. "Tell me what you're wearing," he says when he hears her voice. "Tell me what you're wearing so I can see you perfectly."

Squirrels

After countless phone calls that had gotten her nowhere, Cammy had finally found what she'd been looking for: a man who called himself a wildlife rehabilitator, and said he would be happy to make house calls. Best of all, he wasn't going to charge her a cent to get rid of the squirrels that had invaded her attic a month ago and for one reason or another had not found their way home again. She could hear them now, scurrying around in frenzied circles among the disorderly assortment of things that had been stored up there for years—bags full of out-of-style clothing at least fifteen years old; broken toaster ovens, blenders, and irons; books from college that she'd been planning to reread; incomplete sets of dishes dating back to the beginning of her marriage.

The wildlife rehabilitator, whose name was Gordon McVicker, arrived precisely when he said he would, just a few minutes after Cammy had put her son, Nathaniel, to bed. In one hand Gordon carried a butterfly net, in the other, a pair of soiled-looking gauntlets. He was wearing black jeans, a sweatshirt, and sneakers, and his long, very blond hair was gathered neatly in a ponytail.

"They're driving me bananas," Cammy said, forgetting to say hello as she let him in. "I mean, totally, especially at night, when they're doing their native rituals right over my head."

"So I take it you're thrilled to see me," Gordon said, and winked at her.

"Are you kidding?" said Cammy. "You're my knight in shining armor. Can I get you some zucchini bread or something, or do you work better on an empty stomach?"

Cammy's teenage daughter was slouching her way into the living room, dressed in the turquoise one-piece bathing suit and tights that she wore every night when she did her exercise tape. Her collarbone was polished with perspiration, and the rise and fall of her chest seemed impossibly slow and distinct. Last night she had slept over at her father's, as she had recently begun to do once a week, and had arrived home from school today tired and exasperated, clearly dissatisfied with the familiar comforts she had grown used to. It seemed to Cammy that this crankiness had always been her daughter's mark, like a blaze of white between a cat's black satin ears.

"How're you doing?" said Tina. She shook Gordon's hand and wouldn't let go of it, as if she needed to hold on to him for balance.

"How's it going?" Gordon said.

"Actually," said Tina pleasantly, and dropped his hand,

"I had brain surgery two weeks ago, but they tell me I'm doing just fine."

Cammy let out a sigh through her teeth. "Go to your room and stay there until it's time to leave for college," she said. Tina smiled at this, but remained where she was, arms folded across her chest, one bare foot tapping noiselessly against the carpet. "She's like a child," Cammy heard herself saying out loud. Like a child, Tina kept asking the same questions over and over again during the weeks and months following her father's departure from home. The easy answers Cammy gave her weren't the ones her daughter needed to hear, but Cammy held fast to them anyway, finding comfort in the clichés that came out in a near-whisper, one after another, shamelessly, until at last she could no longer bear the sound of her own voice. "So love comes and goes, is that it?" Tina had said with disgust. "That's it," Cammy said. "And if I have to say it one more time I'm going to shoot myself, get the picture?" That was the day, only a week ago, she realized, that Nathaniel had fallen down a carpeted flight of stairs at his father's house and broken his wrist. Hurling herself through the entrance to the emergency room, Cammy had stumbled into the surprise of her ex-husband's wide open arms, and the two of them had wept together, so long and hard that both of them knew it couldn't simply be the tiny fragile bone of their precious child that they were weeping over. Whatever it was, Len had told her, he could not bring himself to discuss it that day, or any other, preferring instead to leave things as they were—friendly enough, but uncomplicated by passion. "Smart," Cammy had said, nodding her head as if in simple, perfect agreement.

Nathaniel was calling from his bed now, saying he was hungry and wanted a pizza. "And Pepsi," he added. "And Coke."

"Go to sleep," Cammy called back, but a few moments later, he had wandered out into the living room and was standing next to her, blinking at Gordon in confusion. He had gone to bed in pajamas that said "I'm the Big Sister" across the front—hand-me-downs from a friend of Cammy's who had two small daughters. Embarrassed, Cammy swept him up from the floor and hid his chest against hers.

"Who's that?" Nathaniel said, pulling away from Cammy and sliding down to the carpet.

"Actually, I'm a teacher," said Gordon. "Do you go to school?"

Nathaniel shook his head. "I go to Sesame," he said. "And I have a broken arm."

"Really," said Gordon, who dropped down beside him. Delicately, without hesitation, earning Cammy's affection in a single instant, he ran his fingertips along the length of Nathaniel's cast. "My X-ray vision tells me it's healing beautifully," he said.

"I thought you were here about those stupid squirrels," said Tina. "I thought you were the one who was going to knock their heads together and dump them into the trash."

"Don't you know you're not supposed to talk that way to a wildlife rehabilitator?" Cammy said. "He probably has a passion for animals you wouldn't believe."

"True," said Gordon. He told them about the wounded ducks, crows, and geese living in his garage, the raccoons in his den, and that, twice daily, he fed hundreds of wild birds.

"Neat," said Tina. "You must be, like, a very special person."

"That's what my wife used to tell me. After a while, she got tired of the whole deal. The last straw turned out to be the mallard with bronchitis living in our bathtub. Of course, it was only temporary, but it seemed like forever to her."

"On the subject of last straws," said Cammy, "for me it was all those perfumed cards my ex-husband kept hiding around the house. He used to tear them out of magazines and stash them all over the place—in my nightgown drawer, the kitchen cabinets, in between the cushions of the couch. It was Obsession here, Opium there, Chanel No. Five everywhere."

"The man was like, an unbelievable womanizer, that's the major thing," Tina said.

Cammy put her hands to her face. She looked at Tina's smooth blank face, searched it for the slightest hint of regret, and, sighing, gave up. She thought of last year, how her mother had been the day before she died—frightened, bewildered, hands too weak to reach for anything at all. She thought of her mother whispering: *Is this me? I'm so ashamed that this is really me.* Stroking her mother's grayish-white cheek, Cammy had told her, *It's not you. Of course it's not the real you.*

"Anyway, let's talk about something else," said Tina. She smiled at Cammy. "Like, how neat it's going to be to watch those damn squirrels get what's coming to them."

Cammy ignored her. "What are *you* smiling at?" she asked Nathaniel.

"Me," said Gordon, his face hidden behind the butterfly net. "Kids know that looking at me is a cosmic experience." He lifted the net from his face and swooped it down over Nathaniel's, making him laugh.

"More," said Nathaniel. "More more more."

"Greedy little thing, isn't he?" said Tina.

"No more," said Gordon. "It's time to rescue those guys upstairs. How do I get up there?"

"Follow me," Cammy said, and directed him down the hallway that led past three small bedrooms and a bathroom. A short length of braided plastic cord hung from a patch of ceiling outside Cammy's room. Cammy stood on her toes and yanked at it, then stepped back as a half-flight of unpainted wooden stairs tumbled from the ceiling.

Gordon slipped on his gauntlets, waved the butterfly net over his head, and bowed deeply to Cammy, who snapped the heels of her sneakers together in salute as she watched him disappear into the attic.

"The man's not coming back," said Nathaniel, and hung his head. "He's gone."

"Don't be silly," Cammy said. "He's got a couple of hundred birds counting on him for their breakfast tomorrow." She lifted Nathaniel into her arms and kissed the sweet warm skin at the back of his neck. She saw him lying face-down in a tiny heap at the foot of Len's stairs, heard the horrifying silence followed by a reassuring howl, saw Len's dive down the stairs in slow motion, shirttails flying, bare feet gracefully pointed in the air. It had been a week since the fall and Len still couldn't sleep. He envied Cammy's innocence, he told her in a phone call that had begun around midnight and lasted until two.

"The difference between those who have custody of their children and those who do not," Cammy finally said, "is that the 'haves' get up at six no matter what, and the 'have-nots' can do as they damn well please. I've got to go to bed now, Len." Full of apologies, he'd hung up the phone. A moment later, he was back. "I guess I meant to thank you," he said. "For everything." And then he hung up again. When the phone had rung that second time, she'd been poised to say "I love you, too," could even hear, in her mind, the words slipping out in an impassioned rush. She did not call him back. She lay with her cheeks blazing, flat on her back in her lighted room, one arm thrown over her eyes, listening to the sound of her daughter rising for a third trip to the bathroom. On her way back to bed, Tina had peeked shyly into Cammy's room. Crossing the threshold after an instant's hesitation, she'd drawn up the blankets over her mother. Her hands lingered along the satiny edge of the top blanket and then found Cammy's face.

"Do yourself a favor," Tina whispered.

"What?" said Cammy, when her daughter fell silent.

"Don't cry so much in the middle of the night, it's like, not good for you."

"I wasn't crying," said Cammy.

"You weren't? I guess it must have been me, then," her daughter said, so casually and with so little conviction that Cammy had to laugh.

Tina had stood there, skinny in a knee-length nightshirt, feet enormous in furry brown bear slippers decorated with two-inch claws at the toes. She stared at Cammy for a long while. "I don't think I like you," she said at last. "Not much, anyway."

"It's been that kind of night," Cammy said, and vanished under the blankets. She waited for the sound of her daughter's retreating shuffle, claws perfectly silent as they skimmed the carpet. Overhead, the squirrels played hard, and Cammy drifted toward sleep listening to their delicate footfalls in the darkness.

"Heads up, heads up," an urgent voice was saying now. A pair of high-top sneakers dangled briefly from the opening in the ceiling, and then two long legs in faded black denim emerged. "Piece of cake," said Gordon. He hurried down the steps with the butterfly net, his two prisoners barking in utter panic, and flew out the front door with them, Cammy following closely behind. She watched as he set them loose next to the rhododendron, smiled as he murmured words of encouragement and good luck.

"It's back to the wild for these guys," said Gordon

when he saw that Cammy was at his side. He stripped off his gauntlets and tossed them into the frozen grass of Cammy's front yard. "Now all you have to do is put a screen in the chimney."

"Ah, wilderness," Cammy said, stretching out her arms toward the split-levels and small ranch homes that sprouted all around them. Under the street lamps, little Japanese cars and an occasional station wagon gleamed. A neighbor in a down vest smoked a cigarette as his collie peed against the rear tire of a strange car parked in front of Cammy's house.

"Hey, man," Gordon called out. "Thanks a lot."

"Cut it out, Princess," the man said mildly, and nudged the dog forward with his foot. He shrugged his shoulders. "Sorry."

A bright white moon, flat as a drawn circle, sat in a black sky busy with stars. Cammy studied it until her eyes saw only a blur.

"Tired?" Gordon asked. "Cold and hungry and pondering your fate?" He took a step closer to Cammy. "All of the above?"

"How much do I owe you?" Cammy said.

"Forget it. I don't take money and I don't take American Express."

"Did you really sacrifice your marriage for a duck with bronchitis?"

"It was no sacrifice, believe me. It was the mallard that was worth saving."

A small face appeared at the storm door, mouth and nose squashed grotesquely against the glass.

"Get your mouth off of there, Nathaniel," Cammy yelled. The face stayed where it was, steaming up the glass until Cammy could barely see what was behind it. "Dirty!" she yelled. "What's the matter with you?" She ran to the door and flung it open, unintentionally knocking Nathaniel to the floor.

"You said pizza," Nathaniel insisted.

On her knees next to him, Cammy helped him up. She shook her head. "*You* said pizza, baby boy." She held his cast out in front of her, and gazed at the sloppy-looking heart Len had drawn on it in red marker, and the "Love, Daddy" crammed inside it. Bowing her head, she dropped a single kiss against the plaster, and then she let him go. "What kind of pizza?" she asked.

"Cheese," said Nathaniel. "Extra cheese."

"Mushroom," said Gordon, letting the door snap shut behind him. "I can drive you over. It'll be my treat."

"Hold it a second." Tina looked up from the magazine she was reading at the dining room table. She was still in her bathing suit and Cammy could see, as she moved toward her daughter, the light hairs that stood out straight against the gooseflesh of her arms. "You guys want me to baby-sit so you can hang out in some pizzeria? No way. What if the baby falls down the stairs and breaks his other arm? Then what?"

"We don't *have* any stairs," Cammy said evenly, and turned to Gordon. "That's not a bad offer—I think I may actually take you up on it."

"All I know is that I'm not in the mood to baby-sit tonight. That's for sure."

"I'm sorry you feel that way," said Cammy. She carried Nathaniel into his room and changed his diaper. Grabbing him by the ankles as he lay on his back, she clapped the soles of his bare feet against her ears. "You-have-a-bad-and-selfish-mommy-tonight," she sang to him in a whisper. "What-do-you-think-of-that?" Nathaniel hummed a high-pitched tune of his own in response as she got him into a sweatsuit and then slipped his arms tenderly through the sleeves of his ski jacket.

In the den, Gordon and Tina were sitting on opposite ends of the couch watching an HBO comedy special. On the paneled walls around them hung black-and-white photographs in silvery frames—Cammy's father in knickers, top hat, and prayer shawl on his bar mitzvah day, Cammy's mother as an oversized infant looking gravely at the camera from the wicker carriage in which she was posed upright, Len's great-great-grandmother frowning in a kerchief and ankle-length apron. A magazine photo of Bob Dylan and Joan Baez was Scotch-taped over the back of the couch, though Cammy could no longer remember who had put it there or why.

"What's with this guy, anyway?" Tina shook her fist at Robin Williams, who was on the screen talking about natural childbirth in what sounded like a foreign language. "He's no Pee-wee Herman, that's for sure."

"We'll be back in half an hour," Cammy said. "Okay, sweetie?"

"Have the time of your life," Tina said darkly, eyes still on the TV screen. Then, "Just promise you won't forget me."

A teenage girl with alternating red and blue fingernails took their order at the I'm-in-a-Hurry Pizzeria. Cammy stood waiting at the counter while Gordon followed Nathaniel to the video game at the back of the store, lifting him in his arms so the controls would be within Nathaniel's reach. Behind the counter, the chef was sprinkling handfuls of mozzarella onto a finished pizza, and talking loudly to two customers in lumber jackets who were seated at a Formica table up front.

"Look at me," he said. "When I first got started in this business, I was making four hundred a week. Now I'm making two thousand a week, I've got a wife, a girlfriend, a 1987 Caddy, and I speak seven languages."

"Oh yeah?" One of the men put an arm up on the table and sank his chin into his palm. "I used to have a wife and a girlfriend. Now I just have a girlfriend."

"You're lucky," his companion said, shaking his head. "I used to have a wife and a girlfriend, too. Now I have neither."

The teenage girl drummed her red and blue nails against the counter. "You guys are so dumb, you really crack me up," she said. "Only a woman would know how dumb you really are." She smiled at Cammy, who smiled back. "Am I right?"

Cammy looked over at her child, safe in the circle of Gordon's arms, heard and savored his still-babyish laugh of pure pleasure. Walking slowly in their direction, she saw an unfamiliar man down on the living room floor beside her son, saw again how sweetly, how lightly, he had played his fingers along Nathaniel's cast. She imagined his wife, a tall impatient woman emptying her closet into a pair of suitcases, taking one last look at the sickly mallard tamely floating in her bathtub, at the raccoons in the den settled so comfortably on the windowsills. Cammy would never have given up on him so easily. Even after there was nothing left, she would still be holding on. I'm not a life raft, Len had told her, exasperated. You don't want me that way. She could never quite admit that she wanted Len out and finally he had left on his own, doing her the favor that she could not do for herself. For several months she believed that he had been wrong, that she was sinking fast without him; weepy and distracted and unable to take pleasure in anything at all, she felt just as she had when she had learned about the first of his lovers. But she was better now, had been better for a long while. It was clear to her that Len's embrace in the emergency room had been a setback. The warmth of his tears against the side of her face had seemed to her a miracle, something she must have been hoping for all along. But nothing had come of it except this weight of disappointment that had left her leaden and cold and immeasurably lonely. What she wanted was someone to say, *Of course it's not you, of course it's not.*

Nathaniel ran past her, heading for the bottles and cans of soda in the refrigerated glass case. "Open up," he said, thumping his fist against the refrigerator's handle. "Open up, goddamnit."

"I didn't hear that," said Cammy, hurrying to catch up with him.

"Open the door, *please*, goddamnit."

"You can see he's been watching a little too much 'Sesame Street,'" Cammy said as Gordon approached.

"Can I open the door for him?"

Cammy nodded. She waited until he had turned away from her, until she could no longer see his face. "I've been wondering about you," she said.

"Me?"

Nathaniel took a large bottle of Pepsi from the refrigerator and cradled it lovingly in his arms. "Rock-a-bye baby," he crooned, gently swinging his arms back and forth. "Rock rock rock and roll, baby."

"What can I tell you?" said Gordon. "The great animal lover inexplicably flunks out of vet school, becomes a science teacher, buys a little house on the water, takes in a swan with a wounded wing..."

"The usual," said Cammy.

"I'm a happy man," said Gordon. "Give me a crow with sinusitis, let me nurse him back to health, send him back out into the wild, and I'm as contented as anyone can be." He stared at her for a moment, and a look of disappointment crossed his face. "You don't believe me," he said, sighing. "People are so suspicious of happiness, I don't know why. It's as if they want to hold it up to the light and squint at it, turn it upside down and inside out, looking for flaws. Not me."

"So you've given up on them?"

"What? People?" He was staring at her again, this time with surprise. "I'm here, aren't I?" he said. "I could be home hanging out with raccoons and an assortment of winged creatures, but I'm not. I'm here."

"I know your type," Cammy said. "I know you always go out on the town with the lady of the house after springing some squirrels loose from her belfry."

"Always." He touched the sleeve of her jacket. "I mean, never," he said.

When they got back to Cammy's, Tina had changed into a droopy pink terry cloth bathrobe and had set the kitchen table neatly for four. There were linen place mats and matching napkins, and a champagne glass at each setting, their stems ringed with dust from all the years they'd been hidden away at the very back of the highest cabinet.

"What's going on?" said Cammy. "How did you manage to find the champagne glasses?"

"Stood on a chair and snooped around," Tina said. "I figured it was time for a celebration."

"You shouldn't be standing on chairs and you shouldn't be snooping around. It's dangerous," said Cammy. "And what are we celebrating?"

"I don't know, you tell me," Tina said, sounding annoyed. "You never tell me anything."

"Are you all right?" Cammy asked.

"I'm hungry," said Nathaniel. "I want to go to sleep."

Gordon opened the pizza box and tugged at a piece until it finally gave way from the center. He lifted Nathaniel onto a chair. "There you go, kiddo," he said.

"Not *that* piece," said Nathaniel, squinting at the slice on his plate. "What's that green stuff?"

"Oregano," Cammy said. "It makes the pizza taste better. Don't worry about it, it's just a spice."

Nathaniel lifted the slice to his mouth and nibbled at it halfheartedly.

"Keep up the good work," said Gordon. He pulled out a chair for Cammy. "Shall we?"

"Wait a minute," said Tina as Cammy dropped into her seat. She fingered the belt of her bathrobe for a while, and began wrapping it tightly across her palm, like a bandage. "Let's all stand in a circle and hold hands and maybe someone will get married," she said dreamily.

"For crying out loud," Cammy said, but then watched as Gordon, Tina, and Nathaniel arranged themselves into a circle, trancelike and without a word, and then joined hands.

"Come on," said her daughter, and Cammy stood up, taking Gordon's hand and Nathaniel's into her own. "Eyes shut," Tina commanded.

"What is this, a séance?" said Cammy, and was relieved to see that Gordon was winking at her.

Obediently, they all closed their eyes and kept them shut; all except Cammy, who peeked out at Gordon, and studied the slight quiver of his eyes beneath their gleaming lids, the upward sweep of his sparse blond lashes, the faint pale shadows that his lashes cast upon his face. Looking further, she saw hundreds of wild birds at his feet, clamoring impatiently for love. And there she was, a bird of extraordinary size and beauty, simply waiting her turn among them.

Flying

~~~~~~~~~~~~~~~~~~~~
~~~~~~~~~~~~~~~~~~~~

Alice's grandmother's funeral happens to fall on a sweet spring day that would have been perfect for a tennis match or a slow ramble through Central Park. At the cemetery, a nonsectarian place called Gates of Paradise, Alice takes her father's hand and looks over her shoulder to smile faintly at the twenty-five or thirty mourners clustered behind them. The rabbi begins to speak. "According to the one closest to her," the rabbi is saying, "this was a woman who did not inspire much love, a woman who was difficult, if not impossible, to warm to." He pauses, and squints in the glaring sunlight at his audience. "Selfish, argumentative, unforgiving," he continues in a monotone. "Ungrateful—" Alice lets go of her father's hand and kicks him hard in the shins, several times.

"Give the old lady a break," someone calls out in a deep voice, then is shushed into silence.

"Now what, you may wonder, can we learn from a person like this?" the rabbi asks.

"Will you kindly stop kicking me?" Alice's father says into her ear. "I think you may have fractured my ankle."

Alice bolts from the gravesite and runs back to the hearse in her high heels, with Drew, her fiancé, right behind her.

"Well," says Drew, as he and Alice lean against the hearse, both of them breathing hard and pushing their long hair from their eyes. "You know what they say about the truth setting you free."

"I'm speechless," says Alice. "Can you believe my father told the rabbi to say that garbage? I mean, it's true that you couldn't quite love a woman like that, but even so..." She slips off one shoe and wiggles her toes in the warm grass. She thinks of her grandmother, chronically and incurably cantankerous, who always enjoyed a good fight with her son, her eyes glittering as she accused him of failings so numerous it was hard to keep track of them. Once, a couple of years ago, Alice had come through the doorway of her father's apartment in time to hear her grandmother yell, "And in addition to everything else, Victor, you're too short!" After that, it seemed to Alice, her father fought back only halfheartedly, and without much enthusiasm. He no longer had the stomach for it, he claimed. As proof of this, he would stick his hand into his pants pocket and come up with a palmful of Tums, each one chipped at the edges and speckled with lint. "This is what the old lady has driven me to," he'd say, and flip a couple of pills into his mouth, not bothering to inspect them for lint. "This."

Victor is a dentist specializing in adult patients terrified at the thought of walking into a dentist's office. All day long he soothes his patients' fears, talking to them with great sympathy and gentleness. His patients love him, and think he is a miracle-worker. He speaks to them as if they were children, which suits them just fine. Often he talks to Alice the same way, especially when the conversation turns to Drew. Since his mother's death, Victor has seemed exhilarated and full of energy, most of which he spends on trying to convince Alice that the world is overflowing with interesting men, men far more interesting than Drew. "The man works in the garment center," her father says, and shivers. "What am I *supposed* to think of him?" If she marries him, Victor insists, she'll awaken disappointed every morning for the rest of her life. ("With the taste of disappointment on your lips," is how he puts it.)

"I love him," Alice says calmly.

It's been several months since the funeral, and her father has come to her apartment one night after dinner so that Alice can model her wedding dress for him. She spins around in her bare feet in the middle of the living room, taking care not to trip on the gown, which is floor-length and trimmed in lace.

"Don't give me that," says Victor. "You're twenty-five years old and already you're on husband number two. Don't you know how nervous that makes me feel?"

Alice collapses on the couch next to Victor, lays her head on her father's lap. He is wearing tan Bermuda shorts, a button-down shirt, pale blue, with the sleeves rolled up, and loafers without socks. (Her grandmother used to call him "a snappy dresser," the only compliment she ever offered him.) The skin over his knees is smooth and shiny; Alice can't resist whamming her hand just under his kneecap, so that his leg shoots out comically, uncontrollably. "What about the dress?" she asks.

"You're a beautiful girl. Anything you wear looks great

on you," Victor says, rubbing his knee with both hands.

"The truth," says Alice.

"The truth is," says Victor, "the man you're in love with is an unimpressive guy. He's good-looking—I'll give you that—but he's a wimp nevertheless. Besides, you've only known him a day or two."

"Six months," says Alice. "As I've repeatedly told you, the best six months of my life." She cannot help smiling, thinking of the icy winter night when she first met Drew. It was in a supermarket, in the frozen foods section of a narrow-aisled, brightly lit A&P. Alice was there with her therapist and a group of nine men and women, all of whom were on the lookout for love. According to Lorna, the therapist, the A&P was as good a place as any for the group to try out their social skills. They were supposed to approach a person of the opposite sex and make small talk the best they could, no matter how depressed it made them feel. "Confidence is the name of the game," Lorna reminded the group as they trooped slowly past a row of sleepy-looking cashiers. "Feel good about yourself and the world is your oyster."

"Is this a dream?" a fat, freckled cashier asked. He peeked over the top of the *TV Guide* he was reading and rolled his eyes at the group.

The cashier at the next register had a tiny gold cross pierced through his ear and three larger crosses hung from a chain around his throat. "No, man, this is real," he said. "This is New York City, land of opportunity." He hoisted himself onto the empty checkout counter and stood up, raising his arms toward the ceiling theatrically. "Pick me and I guarantee you won't regret it," he said. "Johnston Livingull Seabird: M.F.A., Yale Drama School, New Haven, Connecticut. Not a school for dopes by any means."

Eyes looking downward, Alice made her way to the rear of the store, thinking ungenerously of Roger, her ex-husband. Roger had dropped out of graduate school at Cornell to join a community of Sikhs in Tucson. He had asked Alice to go along, but the thought of herself as a Hindu, her arms and legs tightly bandaged in white, her hair hidden under a turban, seemed as impossible as their marriage itself, which had gradually and mysteriously been emptied of affection, generosity, and patience. All that remained was a sentimental attachment to one another, an attachment not easily broken, she discovered. She and Roger had been high school sweethearts in New York and had married while they were still in college. In the year since their marriage had ended, Alice had moved back to Manhattan and gotten a job in the advertising department of a magazine for businesswomen. Most important, she had made a daily effort to think of Roger as someone who had simply disappeared, like a leaf that had been carried off by the wind. A few weeks before Christmas, she had sent him a season's greetings card. Under her signature, she wrote, "Trying unsuccessfully to savor the pleasures of solitude and independence," but nothing came of it.

Shivering at the frozen food counter, Alice buttoned up her down jacket and stamped her feet a few times, as if to clear them of snow. There was no one in view except a man in a camel's hair coat studying some packages of Lean Cuisine, and a small child in a stroller whose head and face were almost completely covered by a thick, furry raccoon mask. The child was holding a plastic gun cocked to his head.

"Believe me, I know just how you feel," said Alice.

"Kill kill kill," said the child, but listlessly.

"You say that word one more time, Brandon, and I'm going to take the TV set and pitch it straight through the window as soon as we get home," the man warned. He turned to Alice. "Can I interest you in the sale of a three-year-old tonight? A dollar eighty-nine and I'll throw in the stroller for free." Then his expression changed and he was winking at her.

"If you throw away the TV," Brandon said, "you won't be able to watch the Eyewitness News Team ever again."

"Watch your step, wise guy."

Brandon leaned over the side of his stroller. "How're you doing, sir?" he said to Alice. "Slap me five." Alice struck his palm lightly and introduced herself. "Slap me ten," he said. Alice ignored him.

"I'm Drew," said the man. "Overworked and underappreciated, as you can see." He looked at least five years older than she and very tired. His hair was curly and reached to his shoulders; there was an odd, bright patch of silver above one ear. Alice was startled by his face, a beautiful, brooding face that reminded her of Alan Bates in *Women in Love*. She noticed that the rawhide lace of one of his deck shoes was untied. "You're going to trip on that," she said, and immediately had a vision of herself bending over to tie it. She put her hands in her pockets.

"What time is it?" Brandon asked. "I have to watch 'The A-Team' at eight o'clock."

"I hate to break it to you," said Drew, "but it's already more than half over. You're going to have to wait until next week, kiddo."

Brandon lifted the raccoon mask from his face and threw it to the floor. "Daddy?" he said sweetly.

"What?"

"I think I hate you a little right now."

Drew sighed; he and Alice smiled at each other for a moment. "Don't feel you have to apologize," he told his son, "just because you've humiliated me in front of a perfect stranger."

Alice picked up the raccoon mask and struggled to pull it over her head. "I'd like to tell you my life story," she said from behind the mask, "but I'm supposed to limit myself to small talk."

"You mean like who's going to win the Superbowl?" said Drew. "Forget it. I like to get right to the heart of things. Under the right circumstances, I'll tell anyone at all that my wife traded her marriage for the chance to make silver jewelry with some famous craftsperson in Vermont."

"Do you have HBO?" Brandon asked Alice. "If you have HBO, we could come over and watch *Superman III* at your house."

"Would you believe I don't even *own* a television set?" It was getting steamy under the mask; Alice was sure she could feel perspiration trailing to her chin. She peered through the eyeholes at Drew. She liked it that he needed a haircut, that his dungarees were nearly worn out at the knees, and that one of his deck shoes was bandaged with electrical tape at the seams. Men who found themselves unexpectedly alone were no less uneasy than women on their own, Alice thought. Drew looked needy, somehow, and startled, as if he couldn't quite believe the true measure of what he had lost. I don't want this, she'd say out loud to no one each morning those first few months after Roger had gone. Riding the bus downtown to her new job, walking the jammed streets at lunchtime, living without him was all she could think of. Like a child thrusting aside a plate of food, or pushing a mother's hand from the back of her neck, she had thought: *I don't want this.*

Alice watched Brandon, who had kicked off his shoes and climbed out of the stroller, walking the floor with his father's gloves on his feet, looking like some tiny prehistoric creature awkwardly roaming his terrain.

She ran after Drew as he ran after his son, and she thought then of what she was doing—literally running after a man, something she had never done, or ever imagined herself doing. And then she and Brandon were sprawled on the floor, Alice stroking the suede fingers of the glove on the little boy's foot over and over again as Drew stood above them, smiling.

"Sikhs," Victor is saying, and it comes out in a hiss. "With or without that ten-foot-high turban on his head, he was always kind of a wacko. Even when you two were in high school and he came to graduation in that Superman cape, I knew something wasn't quite right."

"You've never said a word against Roger before," Alice reminds him. "I thought you *liked* him. Or at least you said you did."

"My mistake," says Victor. "I must have been concentrating on being polite. You have disastrous taste in men, honey, and believe me, that's putting it mildly. In fact, I get a sick headache every time I think of you and Drew fading off into the sunset." He lifts Alice's head from his lap and swivels around so he can stare directly into her face. His eyes are the most mournful Alice has ever seen. "What kind of man makes it his life's work to manufacture linings for the collars of suit jackets?" he says.

"A pretty successful businessman, for your information," says Alice. She sees Brandon again in the supermarket, hears him saying "I think I hate you a little right now," envying the ease with which he pronounces the words.

After a long silence, Alice says, "The funeral was a disgrace. Unforgivable. I'm surprised the rabbi was even willing to say those things."

Victor shrugs. "It was terrifying to turn against her like that in front of all those people," he says. "But once I got past that, I was flying. I didn't even feel those kicks that were coming at me, all those dirty looks everyone was shooting in my direction. I was flying above those tombstones, soaring, let me tell you." There are tears in his eyes; Alice turns away.

She gets up and takes a handful of pussy willows from a vase that stands on a small pile of magazines on top of a stereo speaker. She holds the branches delicately at her waist and returns to where her father is sitting. "Walk me down the aisle," she says. Her father leans forward, then sinks back into his seat. Alice brushes the velvety catkins against his face. Be happy for me, she wants to say. Or pretend to be happy. It's all she wants from him.

Victor stands and takes her arm. "I'm not making any promises about showing up on the big day," he says. "Not unless you can come up with an acceptable groom in the next few weeks."

"Stately and dignified," Alice says, as they move in small, measured steps from the couch to the piano, no more than twenty feet.

"If I can't talk you out of it," Victor says, "maybe I can convince *him*. Play up all your faults, make you singularly unattractive."

Alice switches on the radio, fools around with the tuning knob until she finds a station that boasts of playing nothing but love songs.

"The first dance is ours," says Victor. He steers her gently around the room as John Lennon sings "Across the Universe."

"There's something I have to tell you," Alice says when the song comes to an end. She checks her father's face, which she has always found sweet-looking despite the sharp chin and small, crooked nose. It is still a face that warms her, reassures her in a roomful of strangers. "Drew has a toothache," she says.

"Mr. Wonderful has a toothache?"

"He didn't want me to mention it," says Alice. "He hasn't been to a dentist in years."

"A dentophobe?" says Victor. "I'm thrilled! Think of the possibilities. I can get him into my chair, buzz the drill right up next to his ear, threaten him with holes in every last tooth until he agrees to do the decent thing and—"

"What's that?"

"Ditch the bride, of course."

Alice pulls away from him.

"Don't look so frightened," says Victor. "You know I wouldn't act in anything other than a highly professional manner."

Alice grabs her father's shoulders. She tries to shake him, as if he were a small child who would yield easily to the weight of her displeasure. But her father stands firm. He looks down at her hands and laughs.

"I'm warning you," Alice says.

"Maybe you'd like a groom with a dazzling smile—a groom with a diamond chip in his front tooth."

Alice disappears into the bedroom without a word. It comes to her then, stepping out of her gown, that she could skip the wedding entirely, cancel the caterer, head for a justice of the peace in some quaint and quiet town not too far up the Hudson. After the ceremony, the strangers who'd be her witnesses would wish her well, then politely turn back to their own lives. A wedding among strangers—she likes the sound of it.

"Call my receptionist in the morning for an appointment," her father says a few minutes later when Alice returns to the living room in her bathrobe. "It's probably a wisdom tooth. People often have trouble with them during times of stress: exam time, divorce time, just before a wedding..."

"Maybe. We'll see." Like her father, she's not making any promises.

"Maybe? How can you be so casual about a tooth in the mouth of the man you love?"

Alice laughs out loud. "What an accusation," she says.

Outraged, Victor's face pinkens; a vein near his eye flickers for a moment or two. "Shame on you," her father says.

Outside the building where Victor has his office, Alice and Drew see a man with a sign lettered on cardboard that says, "Please give $ for caterak surgury for Dusty"— a soiled-looking German shepherd, one of whose eyes is clouded over with a milky-blue film.

Drew pitches some coins into the man's open cigar box. "Best wishes for a speedy recovery," he says.

The man is sitting cross-legged on a plaid blanket next to the dog, reading a newspaper. "Want to buy some dope?" he says in a bored voice.

"Not even a thank-you," Alice whispers. "Do you believe it?"

Drew sighs. "I can't go through with this. The drill, the bright light shining in my eyes, making them tear, all those sharp instruments lined up so neatly on a tray, somebody else's hands poking around in my mouth. I can't breathe just thinking about it."

Brandon is riding Drew's shoulders, high above the Saturday afternoon crowds on Eighty-sixth Street. The three of them enter the small, dim lobby of Victor's building.

"On the other hand," says Drew, "maybe your father will feel differently about me once he's treated me as a patient."

Alice takes his ice-cold hand and squeezes it. In the first few weeks she'd known Drew, she had easily recognized him as someone she would never let go of, a man she would follow to Tucson if she had to. The morning after their first date—a candlelit Kentucky Fried Chicken dinner eaten within earshot of the television while Drew's son stood spellbound in front of it watching reruns of "The Dukes of Hazzard"—Alice had gone out and bought a small TV set for her apartment, as casually as if it had been a box of Brandon's favorite cereal. She was not one for extravagant gestures, not someone who went out of her way to please people, but with Drew and Brandon she grew expansive, sympathetic, indulgent. It was the kind of courtship she had missed the first time around—the relief and gratitude of two adults who had stumbled upon each other at just the right moment. The passion between them bloomed in spite of Brandon, who often seemed to be at the heart of their affair, always, endlessly, needing something: a change of clothes, a bath, a meal, a lap to settle into, a pair of shoulders to ride. He talked incessantly and was astonishingly self-absorbed, and, fortunately for Alice, he wasn't able to see through to her faults. She was the one person in the world he allowed to brush his hair, to change the Masters of the Universe sheets on his bed, to clip tiny silvery crescents from his fingernails. Sometimes, lying in bed on Saturday mornings with Drew next to her and Brandon at their feet mesmerized by a succession of cartoon figures battering each other, Alice thought of Roger and their lost marriage and it seemed that Roger in his high white turban had become a cartoon figure himself, someone she needn't have taken seriously. The betrayal and confusion he had caused were now faint in her memory; all those months of barely getting by seemed only a momentary ache.

"Are you nervous?" she asks Drew. They are backed against a cool marble wall, both of them ignoring the framed directory that lists Victor's name in white plastic letters.

Drew squints at her with one eye. "My tooth is killing me, the thought of your father coming at me with sharp instruments turns my stomach; in fact, even the thought of your father unarmed and relatively friendly turns my stomach."

Brandon raises himself on the tips of his toes and smiles at Alice as he makes a grab with both hands for her breasts.

"What the hell are you doing?" Alice seizes Brandon by the wrists and pushes him away.

"Checking your bosoms," Brandon says, looking insulted.

Alice sighs. "Well, I for one have to say that I feel terrific," she announces. "As if I've taken my life in for a tune-up and..." She stops, embarrassed. Talking this way was unseemly, like boasting about all the money you had in the bank. If Drew didn't feel the same contentment, the same satisfaction that had filled her like a perfect meal, then what? As soon as they met, she had latched on to him with a vehemence that amazed her: dialing his number throughout the day, mostly for the sound of his pleased voice, inviting him over for dinner night after night, then spending nearly a hundred dollars on a television set so that his son would want to visit her. Humiliated, tears come to her eyes. She does not want to need him more than he needs her—that would be intolerable.

"I want a chocolate milkshake," says Brandon. "One scoop of chocolate, one jar of chocolate syrup, all mixed up in the blender for about three days and three nights."

She covers her eyes; tears slide slowly past her palms. She wants to weep against Drew's warm, hard chest, but she will not approach him.

"Come over here," says Drew, moving toward her and pressing her close to him.

"Actually, what I really want is some pineapple juice," says Brandon. "In my special juice cup that I think somebody named Alice gave me."

"The pain," Drew growls suddenly. "The pain." He lets

go of Alice and darts across the lobby into an open elevator, and then is gone.

Drew returns from Victor's office with one less wisdom tooth and carrying a transparent, amber-colored toothbrush that has "Dr. Vic's Magic Toothbrush" printed along the back and front. One of his cheeks is still puffy with Novocain, and he appears to be a little high, giddy with some private pleasure. He cannot stop talking about Victor. "I haven't felt this great in years," he tells Alice at her kitchen table. "What a guy." He smiles, lowers his eyes, notices Brandon lying under the table napping. "Hello there," says Drew, shaking a foot at his son, then, "He's indeed a beautiful person."

"My father's one of the beautiful people?"

"You're not listening to me," Drew complains. "The man has magic fingers." He puts his head down on a woven place mat on the table. "And I'm the happiest guy in the world."

"Magic fingers, magic toothbrush," Alice says. "All in a day's work."

"First he gave me Valium and then we talked about life. He has the softest voice in the world, did you know that?" Drew says dreamily.

"He took psychology courses at the New School."

Drew lifts his head from the table. "I'm flying," he sings. "Look at me, way up high . . ." His head flops down again.

Alice thinks of her father at the funeral, soaring above the tombstones. "You and he, both," she says.

"Goddamn," says Drew. "You know, I think he was pretty impressed with me. He told me I was a wonderful patient, that my teeth were basically in excellent shape, and that it was a pleasure to have worked on me. He did mention, however, that the thought of the two of us get-

ting married gave him acid indigestion." Drew reaches
into his mouth and takes a piece of blood-soaked cot-
ton from deep inside his upper jaw. A bright smear
like badly applied lipstick shines above a corner of his
mouth; Alice bends forward to wipe it away. She
doesn't like to admit that she's even the slightest bit
wounded by what Victor thinks of her future with
Drew. She struggles to remember what it was like to
have a father who was easy to please. Through all the
years of her growing up, and beyond that, past her
marriage to Roger, he had always been sweetly atten-
tive to her, patient and reluctant to find fault. It is
difficult to accept that her father has become unpredictable, someone to be wary of. If she had battled
with him all her life, she would not be feeling as bewildered and vulnerable as she does now. It occurs to her
that perhaps Victor had loved her so unconditionally because he had wanted to steer them away from the rocky
path he had traveled with his mother. Now that she was
gone, nothing looked the same to him: So suddenly Alice
has disastrous taste in men. But what does he think he's
going to do about it? Think of the possibilities, she remembers her father saying, and hears the buzz of an
imaginary drill in the distance. And then she is laughing,
because her stoop-shouldered father, small and slender,
his hands graceful and elegant, has never been a threat to
anyone. Certainly not to the happiness she's charted for
herself—in her mind, a bright arc of endless stars connected across a clear night sky.

She reaches above Drew's head for the phone on the
wall, dials her father's office number. Victor answers the
phone himself. "Dr. Robinson," he says.

"You don't inspire fear in me and that's all there is to
it," Alice says, still laughing.

"Who is this? Would you like an appointment?" her
father says.

"The only thing we have to fear," Drew calls out in the background, "is fear itself. Who said that?"

"Franklin Roosevelt."

"Franklin Roosevelt?" says Victor. He pauses. "Alice, is that you?"

Alice nods her head "yes," and hangs up.

Three weeks later, on a Sunday afternoon as bright as the day her grandmother was buried, Alice and Drew dress for their wedding. With Brandon, they have driven up from the city to New Rochelle, where they will be married on the freshly mown half-acre lawn behind the colonial-style house that belongs to Drew's best friend. Moments before the ceremony is scheduled to begin, Victor arrives, wearing a pale linen suit. "Car trouble," he explains. His face shines with perspiration. He shakes Brandon's hand, nods at Drew, smiles in Alice's direction. He and Alice have not spoken since the day Drew's tooth was pulled.

"What brings you to town?" says Alice. The four of them are hidden from the guests, crowded into the little laundry room off the kitchen, next to an aqua washing machine and matching dryer. In the dryer spins a down vest and a tennis shoe; Alice concentrates on the thump of shoe against metal. From the backyard, the sound of a string quartet playing Mozart can be heard.

"You're my daughter," Victor says. "And that's all the explaining I'm going to do. But don't forget the three L's—live, love, laugh. One of my patients had the words made up for me in fourteen-karat gold and hung them on a chain I was supposed to wear around my neck."

"Lucky you," says Alice.

"Too embarrassing to wear on a necklace, but not the worst advice you could get on your wedding day," Victor says. Then the screen door swings open and the caterer, a middle-aged man in a worn tuxedo, bursts in. Among other things, he is responsible for organizing the ceremony, for getting everyone down the aisle in proper order.

"Bride?" he says.

Alice raises her hand.

"Groom? Ring boy? Father of the bride?" The caterer glares at Victor. "Why aren't you in a tuxedo like your son-in-law?"

"Car trouble," says Victor.

"Great," says the caterer. "Terrific."

"It's a miracle I'm here at all," says Victor.

The caterer rolls his eyes. "It's two-fifteen," he says. "Are we ready to begin?"

Brandon, in gray satin shorts, a round-collared white blouse, and a bow tie, studies the plastic watch shaped like a turtle that's strapped to his wrist. "It's two o'clock," he announces. "Did you hug your child today?"

The caterer disappears out the door, taking Drew and Brandon with him. Soon, the string quartet switches to Wagner.

"They're playing our song," says Alice. She takes her father's arm and guides him out the door, along the white-papered trail that carpets the grass and leads them past the rows of wedding guests seated quietly on folding chairs. More than halfway down the aisle, just before they reach the wedding canopy, Victor abruptly hangs back.

"Pretend you're my patient," he whispers to Alice. "Pretend you're in my chair and listening to the wisest man in the world."

Alice sighs, and kicks him in the shins, gently this time, not wanting to hurt him, but not knowing what else to do.

•   •   •

There are very few relatives at the wedding; nearly all of the fifty guests are friends of Alice and Drew's, and Alice floats among them effortlessly, collecting kisses on both cheeks until they are bright with lipstick. Toward the end of the afternoon she has had too many drinks and knows it; what she would like to do most of all is collapse on the lawn and watch the wedding whirl silently around her.

Brandon streaks by in his underwear and for a moment Alice imagines that he, too, is slightly drunk. "Come back here," she says, and when he approaches her, she grabs him and rests the side of her face across the top of his head. His hair is matted together and smells like pineapple juice. "Delicious," says Alice. "But where are your clothes?"

"Gone," says Brandon. His undershirt and jockey shorts are patterned with tiny superheroes; beneath the shirt Alice can feel the fragile wings of his shoulder blades. "Don't ever leave me," she hears herself say and then Drew is at her side.

"Your father left without saying good-bye," he tells her. "What do you think?"

"Was he limping?"

"Excuse me," a husky voice interrupts.

Alice and Drew turn to see a tall, gray-haired woman dressed in a long wool coat and earmuffs, carrying, in one hand, a plastic bag that says Foodtown, and in the other, a paper shopping bag from Macy's. Both of the bags are stuffed to the top; the sleeve of a purple sweater hangs over the side of the Foodtown bag.

Alice grips Drew's hand in panic. Her heart is thumping, but she doesn't know why.

"Attention shoppers!" shouts the gray-haired woman, and in an instant she seems to have everyone's attention. She puts down her bags one at a time and tosses her coat to the ground, along with her earmuffs and her gray hair. Underneath the wig, her hair is bright blond and soft-looking. She is young and pretty and is now unbuttoning her blouse and getting out of her skirt as a small cassette player at her feet plays music from *The Stripper*. Most of the wedding guests have wandered over to watch, and the men, at least, are laughing and cheering her on. She takes off a white satin half-slip and drapes it over Drew's surprised face.

"Way to go, Drew!" someone calls out.

The stripper is all in black—black lace bra, bikini underpants, black fishnet stockings held in place by a garter belt—but is surprisingly untidy. There's a hole in her fishnet stockings and her underwear is ill-fitting; several dark curls of pubic hair rise above the rim of her bikini bottoms. From one of her shopping bags she removes a ball of tissue paper and unwraps an enormous fortune cookie. Splitting it open, she reads indifferently, "Congratulations to the happy couple from Victor."

There are some hoots of disapproval, but these few voices are overpowered by the men who are applauding and stamping their feet. A couple of Drew's friends seize the slip from his head, and throw it into the air higher and higher until finally it catches on the branch of a lean, curved poplar tree and is abandoned.

Alice cannot look at her husband; she keeps her eyes on the stripper, who, she is startled to realize, looks mournful and pallid. The stripper is heading toward her, her shoulders held back stiffly. Her skin is smooth and pale everywhere. In a trance, Alice reaches out to touch her, her fingertips coming to rest against the soft, pure white column of her neck.

"You don't have to remember any of this," the stripper murmurs. "Just the best parts of things, if you want to."

In the poplar tree, the satin slip flutters for a moment, then drifts soundlessly to the grass.

Snow-Child

Hallie is washing her daughter's hair over the kitchen sink, Delia's favorite place for a shampoo. Delia is seven, and her thick dark hair hasn't been cut in years, mostly because Hallie thinks of it as a treasure, something she wouldn't even consider altering. She gathers it into a towel, twisting the terry cloth so that it looks like a turban perched on top of Delia's head. "Miss America," she says. She passes Delia a long wooden spoon that is lying in a puddle of water on the counter. "Here's your scepter, Miss A."

Delia twirls the spoon under her arm like a baton, splattering drops of water onto the floor. "I unpacked my suitcase," she says. "I took out all the clothes you packed, and put them back in the dresser."

"You goose," says Hallie, but her face is grave as she explains to Delia once again that, no matter what, in an hour or so, her father is coming to take her away for Christmas. It will be the first time in two years that either of them have seen him.

As soon as Hallie finishes speaking, Delia arranges her hands on her hips and thrusts one leg out in front of her. "The problem *is*," she says, sounding to Hallie like an exasperated adult, "I don't want to spend Christmas with *him*. If he wants to see me, why can't he come over for a few minutes and then just go home?"

"It's a court order," Hallie murmurs, crouching down so that their faces are touching, rubbing her thumbs over and over across Delia's fragile ribs.

"Carry me," says Delia, and she seems nearly weightless as Hallie lifts her from the floor, then awkwardly rises. This is her easygoing, soft-spoken child hooked around her waist, flapping her legs hard against Hallie in a full-blown tantrum of grief. (Later, Hallie will discover the lilac-colored bruises that mark her skin and, for a moment, struggle to recognize where they've come from.)

At last they are both in tears.

Jeremy, Hallie's lover, who has been in the bathroom tuning his guitar, rushes into the kitchen, dispensing handfuls of toilet paper to dry their faces. "What a crew," he sighs, watching as Delia lets go of her mother and slides to the floor. "Jesus."

He fixes them frozen French toast in the toaster oven for breakfast and takes Delia's requests for songs. Delia appears perfectly calm, though at the table she climbs into Hallie's lap and says, "First I want you to cut my French toast into eight squares and then I want you to feed them to me." This is a routine she outgrew long ago, but Hallie complies anyway.

"With your *fingers*," Delia says, pushing away the fork

that Hallie has lifted to her mouth. "Feed me with your fingers."

Jeremy plays "Octopus's Garden" and "Rocky Raccoon" for Delia on the guitar, and looks insulted when Hallie says there isn't a song in the world she cares to hear. Jeremy is a music teacher in a private school high up on Fifth Avenue, where he entertains well-behaved girls in dark blue blazers all day. At home, in the apartment he rents with Hallie above a quiet restaurant in the Village, he is constantly humming, like a dishwasher in its final cycle. It has always been difficult for Hallie to tell when he is troubled by something. Sometimes, late at night, lying on the floor with his head in Hallie's lap, he will startle her by saying what a rotten day he's been through. She would never have guessed. The life they share is generally placid and comfortable, and it seems to her a miracle.

By the time Tyler arrives from Massachusetts, where he manages an inn in the Berkshires, Jeremy is at the piano and they nearly miss hearing the buzzer when it rings from downstairs. Tyler is dressed in a tweed jacket and a thick turtleneck, and his pants are tucked neatly into L.L. Bean hunting shoes. He looks thin and drawn, very solemn. He nods at Hallie and Jeremy, and takes Delia by the hand, kissing her a few moments later as an afterthought. Delia seems frozen, her arms held rigid at her sides, her face emotionless.

"I'm no one to be afraid of," Tyler says quietly, and Hallie understands that he is speaking to all of them, but perhaps most of all to himself. She wants to follow Delia and Tyler down the flight of wooden stairs that leads to the street, but Jeremy's hand presses urgently against her shoulder, and she stays where she is, her fists clenched behind her back.

"See you," Tyler calls. Delia says nothing, but shoots Hallie a look of utter resignation—a look meant to break hearts.

Listening to their footsteps on the stairs, Hallie's fists curl even tighter. When the door slams at the bottom of the stairway, she begins to tremble. She can feel her mouth twitching as she speaks to Jeremy. "I must be out of my mind," she says, thinking, in a sudden panic, that it was crazy not to have fought the court order, crazy to have been so generous when, after almost two years, Tyler announced that he wanted visiting rights and to spend Christmas with his child. Last night, talking to him over the phone, she understood.that he had no intention of telling her where he was planning to take Delia.

"I'm a reasonable person," Hallie had yelled into the receiver. "How could I have lived for so long with a lunatic?" She guessed out loud the places where he might go with Delia: His mother's house in Philadelphia? His father's apartment in New York? The North Pole?

"I can't believe it," Tyler said, and she pictured his palm smacking against his forehead. "One chance in a million and she gets it on the third guess."

So Delia is off with her father for parts unknown, is probably heading right now for some remote area of the earth, someplace without telephones or paved roads that can only be reached by dogsled. Actually, Tyler has proved unpredictable over the past few years, and Hallie no longer knows him well enough to even guess at what he might do.

In the kitchen, before she starts on the breakfast dishes, Hallie pulls on a pair of rubber gloves and pushes up the sleeves of her sweater. The gloves, which were a gift from Jeremy, have red polished fingernails, with diamond rings painted across several fingers. She is very fond of them and sometimes wears them around the apartment or when she goes out to the supermarket with Delia, the two of them holding hands, casually swinging their arms for blocks at a time.

The telephone rings.

"The holiday spirit has gotten to me," her mother says when Hallie answers. "I'm calling to offer a little moral support."

"I don't want to talk about it," says Hallie. These days, talking to her mother about almost anything makes her uneasy. This was not always the case. Until Hallie felt the need to confess her affair with Jeremy, the two women had been as intimate as old friends. For the past two years, however, they have kept out of each other's way, phoning twice a month but visiting rarely, even though they both live in the city, several miles apart.

"Don't hang up on me," her mother says. "Just because I happen to believe that a marriage is still a marriage even when the husband can't stay sober for fifteen minutes at a stretch..."

Hallie sighs, and examines the painted jewelry on her fingers.

"...and that adultery is still adultery even when committed by my own previously well-behaved daughter, doesn't mean that I can't sympathize with you from time to time."

"You know," says Hallie, "I've never heard anyone but you use the word *adultery* in a conversation."

"And don't think I've forgotten that he threw furniture at you," her mother says. Hallie doesn't bother to correct her. To Hallie's regret, her mother is the one person she chose to confide in, the one person who knows that Tyler flung a cheeseboard across the room at her, a lovely piece of teak parquet that hit the living room wall and splintered in two. Her mother claimed not to have been the slightest bit surprised. What did Hallie expect, walking around in a daze over some high school teacher just when her husband's need for her was greatest. According to her mother, Hallie's betrayal had to have been "a real shock to the system" for Tyler—as it would have been for any man. She likened it to being fired from a job, number two on her list of terrible blows to the male ego. "You've done him in but good," she told Hallie. Then, softening, "Not that I don't halfway understand."

Her mother had been aware of Tyler's drinking when it began three years ago—had known full well that sometimes Tyler started off the day with a six-pack for breakfast, then had a bottle or two of red wine for lunch, so that by the time Hallie had picked up Delia at school and returned home from work, he had either passed out or was eager for a fight, ready to shield himself from her pity.

Tyler is a photographer who no longer takes pictures, who, in fact, no longer owns a camera. A collection of his photographs, five years' worth, mostly nudes, had been assembled in a book by an art publisher and priced at fifty dollars a copy. It was a beautiful book that for some reason went unnoticed. Tyler was devastated; he lost interest in his work, in everything but drinking and in arguing with Hallie about how much he drank.

At another point in her life she would not have been at all interested in Jeremy, who was seven years younger and had the pinkish, plump-cheeked face of a schoolboy, a face she and Tyler would have laughingly referred to as "well-scrubbed." (Tyler's thick beard and moustache were his only vanities.) But Jeremy appeared one night at a friend's house, self-possessed and sympathetic, a person Hallie daydreamed about even while the two of them stood talking together. She amazed herself by agreeing to meet him at his apartment at lunch hour the following day. Later, in his bed, she felt relieved and happy, and not the least bit confused. Jeremy's lunch hour was just forty-two minutes, which didn't leave much time for talk. But they fit together comfortably from the start, slipping easily into each other's lives, carrying their secret around for months before it began to seem like a burden.

It was two years ago, just after Christmas, that Hallie decided to leave Tyler. She took Delia uptown to her mother's for the night, and arrived home with half of a pizza to share with him for dinner. It happened to have been one of those occasional days when he had sworn off drinking, and Hallie pretended that their sweet, tranquil meal together was a simple pleasure, nothing very remarkable.

"Come over here and sit down next to me and be my friend," Tyler said afterward from his seat on the living room couch. For a moment, in the presence of the old Tyler—good-natured, confident, willing to please her— she began to mourn the loss of her marriage. That he had turned bitter, become impossible to rely on, was the keenest disappointment of her life.

"Tyler," she said, and picked up a small velvet pillow from the couch. She paced the room, hugging the pillow to her chest. "You don't realize what you've done," she said, and told him she was leaving, her voice sounding bewildered and unbelieving.

She watched then, spellbound, as Tyler shot up from the couch, grabbed the cheeseboard from the coffee table in front of him, and scaled it in her direction. But even in her panic as she sidestepped to avoid the flying board, Hallie could see the regret in Tyler's stricken face.

The next minute he was crossing the room in three long strides and embracing her, saying, "I want to win you back." He put his face against hers; it was warm and scratchy, like wool. Then he moved away, and was soon on his hands and knees gluing the cheeseboard together with Krazy Glue. "I have to win you back," he said.

Hallie shook her head at him slowly, wanting to say it was impossible to be with someone whom she had to love and fear at the same time.

"No?" said Tyler. "No chance at all?" He was frowning at the cheeseboard, wiping glue from his hands along the outer seams of his dungarees. He looked up at her. "So I'm already gone. I see in your face that I'm no longer here." He smiled a pained half-smile and held out his hands. "Amazing stuff," he said. "Touch my hand and we're glued together for life." He came toward her slowly, arms raised stiffly in front of him, parallel to the floor, his legs swinging mechanically, not bending at the knee. "It's me, Frankenstein," he said. His voice was soft, a whisper really, a voice he would use to talk about love. "Touch my hand." Their fingertips touched then, but only for an instant, and then, in shyness and confusion, they retreated from each other.

He left that night.

"Those photographs of his were too much," Hallie's mother is saying now, belatedly trying to show where her loyalties lie. "I've looked at that book maybe a dozen times and each time I come away with a three-aspirin headache. Naked women with a hundred bracelets on each arm, naked men in ascots and tweed caps? Maybe it shouldn't be such a surprise to me that things turned out the way they did."

"You know it's a beautiful book," Hallie says. "You're just searching for a way to apologize."

After a while her mother says, "I don't know why I keep coming down so hard on you. But, even after all this time, I still can't make any sense of what's happened: loyalty, respect, love all out the window; Tyler alone in Massachusetts; you and Delia down in the Village with a teenager for a roommate."

"Lover!" Hallie shrieks. "He's my *lover*. And he'll be twenty-nine in June."

"I'm sorry I made you scream," her mother says. "Like any other mother, I only want to see you happy."

Jeremy is at Hallie's side now, slipping a hand into the vee of her sweater. He takes the phone from her and hangs it up. It begins to ring almost immediately; Hallie reaches to answer it before Jeremy can stop her. "Dial two-one-one for credit, and have a happy holiday," she says into the receiver, slamming it back on the hook.

Jeremy takes the gloves off her hands and leads her into the living room, where the stereo is quietly playing a Beethoven sonata, mournful and lovely. It's after eleven now; the restaurant directly beneath the apartment begins setting up for lunch. Chair legs scrape against the floor, and Hallie is lulled for a moment by the indistinct murmur of the waiters' voices as she lies on the carpet with Jeremy close by.

He plants a ring of kisses at her collarbone, places a cool, dry hand over her heart. He looks at her in surprise. "Where are you racing to?" he says, but does not know it is Delia who is making her heart beat faster. A mother, Hallie thinks, is never more conscious of who she is than when her child is in danger. What's the worst that Tyler can do? Hold Delia captive at a drunken party, Tyler himself so drunk that he passes out at her feet, leaving his daughter alone and terrified with a roomful of reeling strangers?

Balancing on one elbow, tapping his fingers lightly on Hallie's stomach, Jeremy hums along with the Beethoven. "You don't have to tell me that this is the worst day of your life as a mother," he says. "You don't have to tell me anything if you don't want to."

She thinks of the night Delia was born, of Tyler dazed from all the joints he'd smoked to calm himself while they were still at home timing the contractions. She remembers the way Tyler's hand shook when he brought the lighted match close to his mouth, then offered her the first toke, a gesture that made her feel so hopeless she'd burst into tears. Of course, Tyler had misunderstood, telling her the pain would be bearable if only she'd do the breathing the way they'd been taught. "You have to listen to me, I'm your coach," he said as he took a drag on the joint, drawing the smoke in noisily.

Hallie had kept score on her own, listing each contraction on the back cover of an old *Newsweek*. In the end, she'd had to call a friend to drive them to the hospital. "I'm freaking out," Tyler whispered to her later as the doctor smiled at them, and Hallie had pretended that her husband was simply in awe at the sight of his newborn daughter.

At this moment, thinking of Delia's birth, Hallie forgives Tyler everything, offering forgiveness in exchange for the safety of her child. It is her child who wanders bewilderedly among Tyler's drunken friends, looking for a way home and finding none. Hallie claps her hands over her eyes, then peeks through her fingers at Jeremy, whose smooth round face stares back at her, alarmed. She's never felt so old, or so uncertain of herself, of the people who fill her life. During these past seven years since Delia's birth, the only constant has been her love for her child, her confidence in herself as a mother. She's heard friends jokingly confess that they weren't "real mothers," by which they meant that they were too often bored with their children, impatient and eager for them to pass through childhood, and begin leading their own lives. For Hallie, Delia's childishness has always been something to be savored—the sweet high-pitched voice saying, "There's a secret I want to whisper to you," then the slender fingers tucking Hallie's hair delicately behind each ear, and the warm breath against the side of her face as Delia begs for two more Oreos, or to watch "Family Ties" just this one time, or to have Hallie lie on the floor beside the bed as Delia drifts toward sleep.

In Delia's presence, Hallie feels like a healer, someone with special gifts, like the woman in her office named Martha, who works as a secretary during the day and spends her nights curing people with her hands. Hallie, who has no faith in such things, and will always remain a skeptic, has no explanation for Martha's success. Not long ago, after suffering for months with a finger that had been fractured in a softball game and never set properly, Hallie allowed Martha to touch her, to warm her finger between her hands. Martha's hands were as large as a man's, and the heat they radiated seemed to have a mechanical source, like an electric blanket that had been turned up to its highest setting. Finding that she could move her finger painlessly, Hallie felt both humbled and angry—a witness to a magic trick, someone who had looked without seeing, and so had been deceived. Yet she feels a kinship with Martha, and sometimes imagines that her own hands grow huge and warm whenever she moves toward Delia—the one person who will always be soothed by her touch.

Jeremy is slipping off her sweater, saying, "There's always this," and she will not argue with him, but will simply stretch out her arms behind her and wait patiently for all the comfort he has to offer.

In the evening, when the phone rings in the middle of dinner, Hallie springs from her chair and flies to the kitchen. "Yes?" she says. Delia's voice is barely audible over the phone. "Talk into the receiver, doll baby," Hallie says. "If you just talk into the receiver, I can hear what you're saying."

"We made snow angels and then a snowman," Delia suddenly shrieks, exhilarated. "Then we went inside and had hot chocolate from a machine. After that, we went to another machine and had Milky Ways and two bags of nacho cheese—flavored Doritos. I put the money in myself."

"Where are you? Where's Daddy? Ask him to tell you where you are." Instead of relief, she feels betrayed by Delia's cheerfulness, her resilience, her easy change of heart. When Delia comes back to the phone, she is giggling. "The North Pole," she says. "We're staying at the North Pole Hilton."

Hallie's breathing is slow and deep. She opens her eyes wide, as if she can see Delia in her hot pink corduroy overalls and plaid flannel shirt. Delia is delicate like her father, but her dark eyes are Hallie's, the whites of them pale blue.

"Daddy says he missed me every day. He called me on the phone for my birthday two years in a row, but we were never home," says Delia. "How come we were never home?"

Of course we were home, Hallie wants to say. "I don't know, sweetie, we must have been out celebrating."

Tyler has taken the phone from Delia. "How are you doing?" he says pleasantly. "Did I say there's absolutely nothing to worry about? Because believe me, it's true. All we did was go out into the snow to build a snow-child. It truly flipped me out, seeing this thing staring at me in the dark. It was so intense, I felt like knocking its stupid head off, you know what I mean?"

"You're high," says Hallie. "Oh, Tyler."

"Not to worry," Tyler says.

"Put Delia back on right now," Hallie orders.

A moment later Delia says, "I'm here, Mommy."

"Jeremy and I are coming to get you." Hallie bites down hard on the tip of her tongue, waiting for Delia's answer.

"Okay," Delia says finally. "But I want to sit next to you

in the front seat, and I want to put my hands in your coat pockets to keep them warm."

"My sheepskin coat?" says Hallie. "That's fine. But first I have to know where you are. No kidding around."

"In the country," Delia answers. "In Daddy's hotel."

Tyler grabs the phone back. "Tell me why you're so disappointed in me. I've stopped drinking, have a fairly respectable job, a fairly respectable girlfriend, and here I am making angels in the snow with my daughter on Christmas Eve. What more do you want?"

"I want to bring Delia home. Just give me directions and we'll come and get her."

"You and your beloved? I couldn't help but notice he's a little on the chubby side. When are you going to put that guy on a diet?"

"Don't," says Hallie. "Just stop right there."

"Am I right?" Tyler is yelling. "You left me for the Poppin' Fresh Dough Boy, am I right?"

"I would have left you anyway." Her voice trails off.

"What?"

"No matter what, I would have left you."

"So it's even worse than I thought," Tyler says quietly, and he seems another person, subdued and disinterested. "Take the Taconic to Route Twenty-three," he says then, and gives her the rest of the directions so quickly, so carelessly, that she has to ask him to repeat them, trying not to sound as if she were frantic.

"Are you sure you've got it right?" Hallie asks him. "Are you sure you're thinking straight?"

"Me?" says Tyler. "I'm no longer the least bit high; in fact, I'm as low as you can go, down in the very sub-basement of despair, brought there by forces—"

"Tell me about your girlfriend," Hallie interrupts, and then is startled to find how deeply she feels a need to cheer him.

"She doesn't hold a candle to you," Tyler says. He falls

silent, then says, "I'm just sitting here by the phone, waiting for a compliment of equal magnitude."

Hallie's mind immediately goes blank. "I'm stuck," she says. "I'm trying to concentrate, but I can't."

"Try harder. Give me something, anything."

She is remembering when Delia first went to school, four years ago, when Tyler's work was still going well and they lived in a loft that also functioned as his studio. Delia was only three, and Tyler would take her to class every day while Hallie went off to work. Delia had been frightened of the other children, who were fearless and noisy, and she had clung to Tyler, begging for him to stay. The teachers had been kind and allowed Tyler to sit at the back of the room, where with great effort he had managed to wedge himself into a child-sized chair every morning for almost three weeks. The one time Hallie had gone to peek in on them, there was Tyler in a miniature chair, his legs nine feet long and stretched out in front of him, crossed at the ankles, his arms dangling to the floor. Looking at him sprawled there so uncomfortably, made patient by love, Hallie had nearly been brought to tears. She never told him that once she had spied on him, that she had studied him for so long, her feet ached from standing on the tips of her toes as she stared through the square of glass at the top of the door.

"Once," she offers now, "you did everything right."

"Not everything," Tyler murmurs, and she imagines the half-smile that is wavering like light across his face.

An instant later, it seems, she is slipping into her sheepskin coat, fishing deep into both pockets for the cool metal of keys. She closes her eyes and sees Delia and Tyler clowning in the snow tonight, sees the two of them grow weary, moving slowly through snow in the darkness, Delia holding on to her father with one hand, balancing herself with the other.

Romance

When he first notices Tammy, she is doing what everyone else at the wedding reception is probably dying to do—dangling her feet in the still water of the circular pool that takes up nearly half the yard.

Russ puts down his plate of salmon mousse and cold pasta salad and sits beside her at the edge of the pool, folding his legs Indian-style. "Outdoor weddings," he says, and sighs. He's come all the way from New York to Los Angeles for his best friend's marriage, traveled the length of the country just to wither and die in this scorching heat. It's one hundred and two degrees and he's dressed in a tuxedo, ruffled shirt, and patent-leather shoes, the most uncomfortable clothing he's ever worn.

Tammy smiles at him sympathetically, and introduces

herself. She stretches her legs out in front of her, then lifts her feet so that her toes are sticking up above the water—small, straight, very white toes with unpolished nails. Her legs are long and freckled, her ankles beautifully shaped. Her face is freckled, too, delicate and pretty. So far, all Russ has gotten from her is a sympathetic smile, but it's enough to make him feel hopeful, as if things are looking up.

"The least you can do is get rid of those silly-looking shoes," Tammy says. "Do you always wear patent leather?"

"I'm highly insulted," Russ says, drawing back from her in mock horror. "Except for my underwear, everything I've got on is rented. Remind me," he says after a pause, "never to agree to be anyone's best man again."

"Certainly," says Tammy. Then she tells Russ that she hates weddings. "I've already had two of my own," she says. "One fancy one and one costume party, which unfortunately turned into a drunken brawl."

He checks to see if she's wearing a wedding ring and is relieved to find that she's not. "And after the costume party?"

"The marriage went straight down the tubes," she says, swiftly lowering her feet beneath the surface of the water again.

There is a woman approaching them now, an older woman who, Russ sees, strongly resembles Tammy. She has the same streaked dirty-blond hair (though hers is cut short), the same graceful neck and pointed chin. She is carrying two unopened packs of cigarettes and a single plate of food.

"Please don't get up," she says. "I'm May Louise, Tammy's mother."

He stands to shake her hand.

"Hot hot hot," says May Louise. "And like a fool, I'm all in silk."

"That's nothing. The best man here is in his patent-leather dancing pumps," says Tammy.

"Please," Russ begins, and can feel his face going red. Turning to May Louise he says, "They're rented, and not a reflection of who I am at all." He sits and pulls them off, along with his socks, then rolls up his pants and eases his bare feet into the water, careful to steer clear of Tammy.

"So whose side are you on?" May Louise asks him.

"The Communist rebels?" he says, hoping for a laugh.

"The bride's or the groom's?" May Louise says, shaking her head at him. "We're from the groom's side. Tammy and I worked with him down in Atlanta before he got promoted and was transferred out here. Actually, though, it was Tammy who was Nelson's friend, and Tammy who got the invitation to the wedding." She goes on to explain that she and Tammy never leave town alone, that neither of them travels anywhere without the other.

"Never?" Russ says.

"It just wouldn't feel right," Tammy says. "May Louise would have been all alone in the apartment, and I would have gotten lonely just thinking about her being there."

"We live together," says May Louise. "Our second divorces coincided exactly, so it seemed to make good sense to have Tammy move right in with me. No point in our paying rent on two separate apartments."

Ross nods his head as if he understands, which he does not. He tries to imagine his mother and sister working in the same office, sharing an apartment, meals, and who knows what else. One dinner in a restaurant together and the two of them are at each other's throats, unable to agree on even the weather beyond the windows. Just because I love you doesn't mean that I have to like you, he can remember hearing his sister shout to his mother, or maybe it was the other way around. He'd suspected that most mothers and grown daughters were like this, fated to disappoint each other in a thousand predictable ways.

He looks first at Tammy and then at May Louise, the two of them smoking cigarettes, blowing smoke peculiarly from the sides of their mouths, tapping their fingers against the tiled edge of the pool in time to the band's music. In only a few minutes, the Victor Velvet Band has gone from early Beatles to the tango and back to rock and roll again.

"Lindy?" says May Louise, reaching to grab Tammy's hand. Her shoes are off now, too.

Long white feathers of smoke floating behind them, Tammy and her mother are off to the dance floor, a small wooden platform constructed by the caterer early this morning. Russ watches as they fling each other about expertly, heads touching as they dip forward, eyes closed in concentration. Inevitably, in no time at all, the other dancers have made way for them, retreating to the boundaries of the platform so that Tammy and May Louise become the focus of attention. They are, Russ has to admit, terrific together, extravagant out on the dance floor, yet in perfect control. The spectators are clapping hands, shouting words of encouragement. At the pool, at a distance, Russ feels half his age, a misfit teenager deserted by his buddies, who have gone off and found just what they've been looking for all their lives.

The three of them are staying at Nelson's house for a couple of days after the wedding, along with some out-of-town relatives and Nelson's teenage daughter and stepdaughter, Jennifer M. and Jennifer R. The two Jennifers aren't on speaking terms, and they stay hidden in their rooms on the third floor, avoiding each other and everyone else. Russ feels sorry for them both. He wishes there were something he could say to lighten their misery, but behind closed doors they are unapproachable. Poor Nelson will have his hands full when he comes back from his honeymoon next week. Nelson has become a very rich man, judging from the size of his house and the miles of wall-to-wall carpeting that follow you everywhere you go. Nelson is vice president of a nationwide chain of motels. Russ has known him since high school, where Nelson was voted "Most Enthusiastic." Enthusiastic about what, Russ had wondered. (No one, not even Nelson, could guess what the title had been referring to. "Life?" Nelson had said, shrugging his shoulders. "How the hell do I know?")

Russ had been voted "Most Likely to Succeed." He was an impeccable test-taker, but unathletic and round-shouldered, an awkward dancer. He was also extremely cynical. Nearly twenty years ago, when he was still a teenager, he believed that the world would be destroyed by nuclear war, that not a single woman would ever fall in love with him, and that high school was an utterly ridiculous place to be. Now—one failed marriage and many love affairs later—he is only slightly less cynical. He is the manager of a rare books shop in Greenwich Village, and lives close by in an apartment filled with cast-off furniture from the house he grew up in—a worn, curved-back velvet sofa; a vinyl lounger permanently tilted toward the ceiling; an ornate breakfront cluttered with books, magazines, dishes, and silverware. His clothing is neatly folded away in file cabinets that were about to be discarded by the bookshop before he rescued them. The apartment suits him just fine, but last night, after the wedding, roaming through Nelson's huge, carefully furnished house, he was aware of a flicker of pain, sudden and sharp, that could only have been envy.

Nelson's house is unmistakably the house of an adult, a person with credit cards and ironed shirts and a secret drawer containing a will and insurance policies. This is a person who has acknowledged the passage of time, who no longer remembers, as Russ does, the exact order of all the songs on the Beatles' *White Album* and Dylan's *John Wesley Harding*. No Levis with shredded knees in Nelson's closet, or posters of John and Yoko Scotch-taped to the walls of his bedroom. After the birth of his daughter, Nelson told Russ, he'd immediately stopped jaywalking across busy streets, a dangerous habit that no parent in his right mind ought to indulge in. Russ was very touched by this, yet also amazed: His oldest, most beloved friend's life was unimaginable to him. After the wedding, Nelson took off for the airport in a rented white Rolls-Royce, complete with a uniformed chauffeur. The two Jennifers stood silently at the curb as the Rolls disappeared from view. Russ briefly held an arm around each of them, but then the girls bolted, almost at the same moment, and flew into the house. He hasn't seen either of them since, though with his ear pressed against the doors of their rooms, he's heard the muffled sounds of weeping.

As he stands in front of the bathroom mirror halfheartedly slapping borrowed English Leather against the sides of his neck, Russ begins to laugh—he's never worn cologne in his life. What is he doing? Tammy and her mother are waiting for him downstairs, ready for an evening at Disneyland, where none of them has ever been before. Earlier in the day, at the pool, when he'd invited Tammy to go with him, she'd nodded, then called out to her mother, "How does Disneyland sound to you?" It turned out that Disneyland sounded great to her, too. Russ was caught off guard: He stood there squinting in the sun, absolutely speechless. Finally he had steered Tammy into the kitchen and explained that he'd been asking her out on a date. Tammy stared at him, then burst into laughter. She hadn't been on a date in five years, she told him, still laughing. He waited for an explanation, but none was offered. He couldn't help noticing how lovely she was with her hair a wet tangle around her face.

Through the sliding glass doors he'd looked out past the patio to the pool, where May Louise was floating by on a speckled Styrofoam board. She was on her back smoking a cigarette, an ashtray resting on her stomach. Her body was long and slender, like Tammy's, looking very impressive in the strapless bathing suit she was wearing, which for some reason Russ found disconcerting. Tammy was born when May Louise was only sixteen, they'd told him at the wedding. Not exactly a marriage made in heaven, May Louise had said, to which she and Tammy had snickered and rolled their eyes. Watching them, their movements in perfect synch like well-rehearsed actresses, Russ was weak with loneliness, the loneliness of an intruder. He was overwhelmed, but only for a moment, by everything that Tammy and her mother shared, the lives they lived side by side.

Car keys in hand now, he rushes down the spiral staircase to the first floor, then slows his steps. Under the staircase is a landscaped area containing smooth gray pebbles and a rubber plant with polished leaves. Jennifer M., Nelson's daughter, is seated there, like a child in a sandbox, sifting through stones.

Russ kneels beside her. "Hi," he says cautiously.

"Please don't talk to me."

"I wouldn't even consider it," he says. "I was just wondering if you'd be interested in a trip to Disneyland."

"Been there," Jennifer says. "At least one hundred and thirty-seven times."

"Got any recommendations?"

"Yes," Jennifer answers, narrowing her eyes. "Stay

home." She studies the single stone in her palm, then closes her fingers over it and hurls it, aiming for the clerestory window fifteen feet above her head.

"Missed!" Touching her arm lightly, Russ adds, "But I wouldn't even *think* about doing that again."

Jennifer strokes a leaf of the rubber plant. "I've re-named myself," she says, and falls silent. "Guinevere," she says at last.

He nods his head, trying not to smile.

"Wife of King Arthur, mistress of Sir Lancelot."

"Well, here's to your new name," says Russ. He raises an empty hand in salute. "Use it in good health."

"Thanks."

"That's a fairly sophisticated name, actually. How old are you these days?" he asks her.

"Fourteen. And if you really want to enjoy yourself at Disneyland, smoke some dope before you go. But you have to be careful. The people who run that place are so straight you can get panicky just looking at them."

"Fourteen," says Russ sadly.

"Thirteen." She smiles at him for the first time, a gen-erous smile that reveals a mouth cluttered with braces.

Tammy and her mother emerge from the family room that opens off the hallway where Russ and Jennifer are seated. May Louise is in jeans and carrying a large straw bag that says "Trinidad & Tobago" on it in different col-ored threads. She has an expensive-looking camera hanging from a leather strap over one arm. Tammy is wearing black shorts and a T-shirt with rolled-up sleeves. There's a sealed, see-through plastic pocket over one breast that's filled with sand and a miniature pair of sun-glasses. The shoes she's wearing are flat-heeled and made entirely of silvery-blue plastic.

"Punk city," Jennifer whispers to Russ.

"I've got a car right out front," Russ says. "No air-conditioning, I'm sorry to report. I guess when you ask for a sub-compact, they assume you can do without luxuries altogether."

"Let's take our car," Tammy says. "It's only a little Toyota, but at least it's cool."

Russ ends up in the backseat, with his knees jammed up to his chin.

"How are you doing back there?" Tammy asks from behind the wheel.

"I'm just so excited about this trip," says May Louise. "To me, Disneyland is like the Pyramids, the Eiffel Tower; you know, one of those mythical places on a post-card that you never think you'll get to."

"Don't be too sure about anything," Tammy says. The car is stopped at a stop sign on an exceptionally hilly street not far from Nelson's neighborhood. "Damn," yells Tammy. "Why do we keep rolling back every time I try to get in gear?"

"Do you want me to drive?" Russ asks. He sees himself vaulting over the top of the seat and landing gracefully in Tammy's lap.

"Honey," says May Louise, "look here, I'm going to put the emergency brake on, then release it as soon as you've given it lots of gas."

Russ leans forward in his seat. He's never seen two people drive a car together before. And so calmly, too. Not an ill-tempered word passes between them. In a moment, they're moving smoothly again, heading for the freeway.

"Well done!" May Louise cheers. "If I do say so myself." She puts two cigarettes in her mouth, lights them, and passes one to Tammy. "So what do you think of Nelson's new wife?"

"Real pretty," Tammy says. "Gorgeous dress."

"Second marriages are so hopeful," says May Louise.

"I mean, you're dying for things to work out well, praying your hardest that you won't screw up like you did the first time."

"Hah," says Tammy, then she and her mother laugh.

If he were alone with Tammy now, Russ thinks, he would ask her about her divorces, try to find out whether her ties to her mother were the cause, or the result, of those failed marriages. He'd like to press a button and eject May Louise painlessly through the roof of the car. Nasty thought, which instantly makes him feel guilty. Trying to work up some sympathy for her, he imagines May Louise as a young, reluctant mother, horrified to discover herself out of high school, living with some teenage boy who works in a grocery store or gas station, the two of them stunned by the life they've been forced to make for themselves, the endless accommodating, the enormity of what they've lost.

"Fantasyland," May Louise sings out as they approach the exit for Anaheim. "Tomorrowland. Adventureland." She hugs herself, confessing that even the names give her the shivers.

"It's just an amusement park," Tammy says, sounding a bit exasperated.

"Indulge me," her mother says. "You know I'm the biggest baby in the world."

Tammy swings the car into a space in the middle of a vast parking lot, which is surprisingly crowded, considering it's nearly sundown. The air has cooled slightly, and there's even a faint breeze. Exhausted-looking families are trooping back to their cars, wearing mouse ears and trailing balloons that are tied to their wrists. "I ought to have my head examined," a man hollers at two little boys holding hands. "You can forget about Knott's Berry Farm and the Dodgers game, too. As of this moment, I'm no longer speaking to you guys."

"There are two ways to do things in this world," May

Louise says loudly. "First class, and with children."

"Listen to the lady," the man tells the two boys. "You hear that?"

At the main gate, while Tammy and May Louise fumble through their wallets, Russ buys tickets for all three of them.

"I absolutely cannot allow it," May Louise says, and thrusts a ten and a five at him.

"Forget it," says Russ, waving away the money. He's feeling very self-possessed. Let her owe me something, he thinks. Let her feel guilty for throwing obstacles in the path of someone who has proved himself to be more generous than she.

"Well," Tammy says, "I guess I'm going to be gracious about this, after all."

"Nothing wrong with being gracious," Russ says. "It's nothing to be ashamed of."

They're walking along Main Street, which is lined with souvenir shops and snack bars, and has a horse-drawn trolley traveling down the center. May Louise is the first to spot Minnie Mouse standing near the louvered doors of an old-fashioned saloon. She's wearing a polka-dot dress, and her hands are huge and white-gloved.

"Minnie!" May Louise calls. She rushes to her side, Tammy and Russ dragging after her. May Louise wants to have her picture taken with Minnie Mouse.

"Don't think I'm not dying a thousand deaths," Tammy says in Russ's ear.

Russ takes the camera May Louise hands him, focuses, and snaps a picture of her with her arm around Minnie Mouse.

"Now you two," May Louise orders.

Russ tries to put his arm around Tammy for the picture, but Minnie Mouse squeezes between them, laying

her arms heavily across their backs. "It must be swelter-
ing inside that costume," Russ says. No response. Minnie
Mouse, he realizes, is playing mute, having taken a vow
of silence to avoid the million witless conversations she
would otherwise have to face every day. "I understand
perfectly," Russ tells her, and watches as Tammy pats her
black plastic nose.

They decide to have dinner in an open-air café on a
street that's meant to be in old New Orleans. The wait-
resses are in floor-length aproned skirts, which, like the
food served, seem to have nothing to do with New Orleans at all.

"The man was a genius," May Louise says as she takes
a bite of her tuna sandwich.

"What?" says Tammy.

"Walt Disney, who else. This place is immaculate, not a
gum wrapper or a cigarette butt in sight. Aren't you impressed?"

"By cleanliness?" Tammy asks. "What are you talking
about?"

"I'm talking about a man who had a dream."

"You're all confused," Tammy says. "That was Martin
Luther King."

"I see," May Louise says coolly. "Please don't feel obli-
gated to humor me just because, in my old age, I need
desperately to be humored."

"This is a fifty-year-old woman you're listening to,"
Tammy tells Russ.

"Well, sometimes it feels like my old age," says May
Louise, and then fireworks begin exploding overhead.
Under the table, Tammy lightly squeezes Russ's knee.
But by the time he looks up, her hand is already gone,
and he tries to remember the feel of it, whether it was
warm or cool against his skin.

She takes his hand and leads him away from the table
toward the picket fence bordering the restaurant. They

stare at the illuminated sky, where a shower of green and red stars appears, only to pale and then fade completely. One explosion follows another; soon they are taking the view for granted, as if the sky will always be this way, always full of surprises.

A man's cheerful voice, probably tape-recorded, announces over the loud speaker that the show is over. Everyone in the restaurant seems to sigh at once. But the cheerful voice promises that a spectacular parade down Main Street will begin in exactly thirty minutes.

Russ's face is still tipped upward, but all that remains in the sky are colorless streaks left by the fallen stars.

"Let me tell you what happened while you were gone," May Louise says when they've settled back in their seats. "A gentleman dressed in a pirate's costume asked me to light his cigarette. He was young and very handsome, and he had a sword at his waist."

"And you let him get away?" Tammy smiles at Russ.

"Not my type," says May Louise. "Anyway, look who's talking." To Russ she says, "Did you know my daughter has men falling at her feet day and night? At the office, she's known as a real heartbreaker, not that any of them gets to share more than a paper cup of coffee with her down in the employees' lounge."

In the gaslight of the café's lamps, Tammy's face glows pink. "May Louise just loves to go and air her dirty laundry in public. Given the opportunity, she'll go on for hours, there's no stopping her. If you're lucky, she might even tell you what a torment it is to live with me, what a slob I am, leaving underwear soaking in the bathroom sink for days, deliberately putting potato chip crumbs between the cushions of the couch, refusing to make my bed except on weekends."

"I don't mind that you're a slob, baby," May Louise says. "It's only a venial sin, after all." She blows smoke in a column that rises straight above her head.

Pushing his chair away from the table, Russ says, "We probably ought to head for Main Street if we don't want to miss the parade."

May Louise looks at him as if he's just suggested that the three of them step out of their clothes and march naked through Disneyland. She is mumbling something he can't understand. "I'm sorry?" he says.

"I hate parades," May Louise says through her teeth. "I'd rather just sit here and sulk all night, if you don't mind."

"Sulking under the stars," says Tammy. "Maybe you'll meet a fellow sulker and the two of you will fall in love right here in Walt Disney's Magic Kingdom."

"Don't laugh," says her mother. "The possibilities for romance are infinite. May I suggest that the sooner you realize that—"

"I put those crumbs there out of pure meanness," Tammy says. "I turned the bag upside down and shook it until it was empty."

May Louise doesn't change her expression. "Fortunately, that Dustbuster I bought myself for Mother's Day works beautifully."

Russ begins to slip easily into the space Tammy has left open for him, in the distance she has put between herself and her mother. There's room for him now, of that he is certain. But he has come to like May Louise after all, and no longer has visions of her sailing through the roof of the car. Instead, he puts her in the backseat of a white Rolls-Royce, her head leaning against the hard shoulder of the man in the pirate's costume.

"What do you want from me?" Tammy asks. There's a salad fork in her hand, and she is pointing it in May Louise's direction.

"I want you to let go of whatever it is you're holding onto so stubbornly," her mother says.

Tammy sighs; this is too much to ask of anyone. "I

only want to live an uncomplicated life," she says.

"Not me," says her mother after a moment. "In fact, if that pirate shows up again, I intend to be a lot friendlier this time around."

Russ looks away, wanting to apologize for eavesdropping, as if Tammy and her mother were strangers at the next table whose whispered confessions he'd been struggling to hear all night. He's waiting to be accused of rudeness, of having overstepped the limits of decency. But no one accuses him of anything; it's as if he's not there at all.

He clears his throat. "I keep thinking it would be crazy to miss the Matterhorn, Space Mountain..."

"I'm afraid the Magic Kingdom has done nothing for me," says May Louise. "I'm bitterly disappointed."

Tammy slides the car keys to Russ across the table, saying she's too tired to drive back to L.A. They are out of their seats in an instant, walking three in a row in silence, looking like members of a family who have already said too much to one another. From the main gate they take a tram through the parking lot; at the car, Russ helps May Louise into the back, then sinks behind the steering wheel.

"Thank you for being so patient," Tammy says.

He doesn't feel patient; he's been waiting forever to have Tammy beside him in the dark. "You can rest your head against me if you're tired," he says.

Tammy shuts her eyes. "You're trying to get close to someone who can't be gotten close to," she says in a small voice, but they're close enough now that their thighs are touching, and then, inexplicably, her head falls across his shoulder. They do not speak again and he realizes, once they are on the freeway, that she has fallen asleep, that he is the only one in the car who is awake. He lifts one hand from the steering wheel and drapes his arm carefully over her shoulder.

He's driving along dreamily, slow as a man lost; the car behind them in the fast lane sounds its horn, flashes its high beams, urging him on. Pressing forward, he hits seventy-five, then eighty, imagining that they are flying, traveling faster than light, so fast that they are invisible.

At home, after Tammy and her mother have gone silently to bed, Russ seats himself at the kitchen table, where Jennifer R. and Jennifer M. are sprawled in their nightgowns, surrounded by empty beer cans. Both of them are drunk and sleepy-eyed, giggling sweetly as Jennifer R. tries over and over again to light the partially smoked joint she's holding in a pair of tweezers.

"You silly moose," Nelson's daughter says, reaching out for the tweezers. "Give me that."

"Goose," Jennifer R. murmurs, and finally lights the joint. She appears to be slightly older than Nelson's daughter, though maybe it's just the impression of white shadow that's brushed across her eyelids, the reddish-brown lipstick at her mouth.

"Now which one of you is Guinevere?" Russ says. He searches through the beer cans until he finds one that isn't quite empty. In his mouth the beer is warm and sour, but he swallows it anyway.

"Guinevere?" The two Jennifers stare at him blankly and laugh, their drunken camaraderie filling him with sadness, which settles in his chest like something leaden, rock-hard.

"Wife of King Arthur, mistress of Lancelot?" he says. No one answers him, and he turns away, looking beyond his shoulder at the pale net of smoke that hangs motionless above him. Tammy, he thinks, and then he envisions their photograph: the two of them separated forever by a mute stranger, a mouse in white gloves. It is Tammy who will one day frame the picture between her fingers, raise it to the light, then draw it nearer and nearer to her face, squinting in confusion. As he turns back toward Jennifer M. and Jennifer R. now, he thinks of himself half-remembered, or perhaps not at all, smiling out at Tammy from a photograph that he will never see.

Away from the Heart

I'm giving the baby a bath in the white plastic tub that's parked across the bathroom sink, looking like a small boat going nowhere.

"How do we raise our hand in school, Sarah?" I ask, and tickle the baby under her arm as her hand shoots obediently upward. "Very good," I say, tickling her some more. She tips her head back and laughs hard, as if she's just heard something hilarious. Watching her, I savor a moment of deep pleasure before giving in to extravagant laughter that brings me to my knees. On the bright bathroom tile I rock back and forth, wheezing and snorting, until finally, inevitably, I retreat into silence, breathless and a little stunned at having lost control like that.

"Oh, Bobby," I hear myself say. I'm busy with the baby now, soaping her perfectly straight back, her pot belly, running the washcloth under her neck and down both plump shoulders. It's been nearly a year since Bobby took off for Florida with his lover. He left me on the hottest day of the year, one day before my thirtieth birthday. Although I had no intention of dying just then, when I awakened the next morning, I found myself fantasizing about what would be said at my funeral. I wanted to be remembered as someone who was never a complainer despite her losses. Closing my eyes, I could hear the minister praising my resourcefulness, my ability to get by in New York without a husband, a VCR, or a walletful of credit cards. The minister didn't know it, but I'd lost it all to Stephanie Sugar, a gracious and sympathetic twenty-year-old who would later send me postcards from Key West, wanting me to know that she was thinking of me and wondering how I was doing. I never wrote back because that would clearly have been too much, but the postcards kept coming all the same, and every now and then it occurred to me that I was grateful for them.

"Out?" says Sarah. She rises to her knees and thrusts both arms in the air.

"Out of the bathtub and into the fire," I say as I lift her from the water.

"Nah," says the baby, and she smacks her palm against her forehead in a gesture of exasperation. She is fifteen months old—a child of such sweetness and good humor that even strangers on the street find her irresistible and are drawn to her side without quite knowing why. Only Bobby was able to resist her; distracted, I guess, by Stephanie's delicately shaped hands, her quiet, high-pitched voice, her faintly apologetic manner, so much like my own. They fell in love shortly after the baby was born, when I was at my worst—exhausted, bewildered, my body soft as a down-filled pillow, my breasts leaking milk through my shirts. Bobby left just before the baby learned to smile. For a long time I thought that if only he hadn't missed that—her very first blossoming—he would never have been able to leave. When I told this to him over the phone, long-distance, he simply fell silent. "I can't," he said finally, and sighed into the receiver. "I mean I can't even begin to figure out where you come up with these things."

"Mom," the baby says. "Mah mom." Her legs are clamped around my waist, her moist cheek fastened devotedly against mine. We stay that way, in heaven, in love, for what feels like a long while, and then, without warning and without apology, she pees on me.

Pushing Sarah in her stroller along the littered streets of upper Broadway, I slow to a stop in front of a store window where mannequins wearing the heads of donkeys, cows, rabbits, and sheep are dressed in the latest sportswear. "Pretty neat," I say to my daughter, and, sighing, wipe the perspiration from the back of my neck. I have to admit that the heat has gotten to me this summer, that all summer long I've moved slow as an old lady through the rooms of my apartment, ignoring most of the housekeeping, but frowning hard at the clutter, as if that were all that was needed to make it disappear.

"Hi," the baby says shyly. "Hi there?"

"Hi yourself," I say as I wheel the stroller into the boutique. I go through the racks of clothing absently, without interest. I think of Bobby and Stephanie Sugar standing together in my living room, the only time I ever saw them together, the two of them standing over the baby while she slept in her bassinet, her behind slightly raised in the air, arms stretched out in front of her. "What a little love," murmured Stephanie. She was there, she said, because she wanted me to see that she wasn't someone awful, someone who went around wrecking other people's lives without any thought at all. "I'm sure you gave it a lot of thought," I said. "I want you to know how much I appreciate it." Stephanie looked unhappy at this, as if she suspected that I had been mocking her. "Honey?" she said, tapping my husband on the shoulder. "We've got to get a move on, honey." In Stephanie's ear there were three earrings, one each of gold, diamond, and pearl. Fingering the diamond, she turned away from my husband and smiled at me. "Thank you for letting me come through the door," she said. Still smiling, she told me that Bobby had said many good things about me, but I couldn't imagine what they might have been. Only a few days earlier, Bobby had criticized me for not being "a real person," which he defined as someone who could cook a decent dinner every night, drive a stick-shift, and change a sleeping baby's diaper in the dark without waking her. It was true that I couldn't do any of those things, at least not with any confidence or expertise. I had a degree in Comparative Literature and could talk about books with insight and enthusiasm with my students, but I could not change a sleeping baby in the dark. "So what?" I had yelled at Bobby, hating him for making me feel ashamed. "Why does that make me any less of a person?" I hollered. "I'm just telling you the way things are," he said, still keeping to himself all the rest of it—that somewhere in the city there was an impossibly young woman who called him honey, so gently, so expectantly, that tears would spring to my eyes at the sound of it.

"I'd like the striped shirt that jackass in the window is wearing," I tell the saleswoman approaching me now.

"You've lost me," says the saleswoman, who is very pale

and very pretty and looks a lot like David Bowie. "I'm not following you at all."

"The donkey in the pink-and-white striped shirt," I say. "The one with his arm around the cow."

"Ohhh," says the woman, looking toward the display window. "And here I was thinking you're on drugs or something. I'm thinking, this person is a space cadet, for sure."

"First impressions," I say, and shake my head.

Halfway down 107th Street, just before I reach home, my path is blocked by a street musician standing along- side the open case of his electric guitar. A handful of nickels and dimes gleams against the maroon velvet that lines the case. The musician is tall and emaciated-look- ing, dressed in black. There is a bit of toilet tissue stuck to his upper lip, at the point where he'd probably cut himself shaving this morning. The man is in a daze, strumming the same minor chord over and over again. Impulsively, I empty my change purse into his guitar case.

"I don't know why I'm bothering to say this," I tell him, "but go get yourself something to eat, okay?"

The musician goes on with his playing. "All mothers are mothers from hell," he sings in a monotone.

"Don't give me that," I say, bending over to cover the baby's ears with my palms. Sarah pushes me away in- stantly, and jams her bare foot into her mouth. She sucks on it a while and then gives it up, her foot making a small popping sound as she pulls it out of her mouth. In the fierce sunlight, the tiny foot glistens with saliva.

At the entrance to my building, I put myself in reverse and pull the stroller backward up the pair of brick steps leading to the courtyard. The usual crowd of teenage boys is having its afternoon smoke, filling the courtyard with the sharp, sour smell of burning pot.

"Hey, how's it going, how're you doing?" one of them calls out to me.

"I'm not speaking to you, Curtis," I tell him. "You know how I hate it when I see you with all those pot-heads."

Two women, both of them old enough to be my students, hold the door open as I struggle to lift the stroller over another set of steps and into the lobby.

"You aren't going to carry that all the way upstairs, are you?" one of them asks. She is the smaller one of the two, and ghostly pale except for the bruise-colored half-moon under each eye. Her short straight hair is bleached nearly white, and she is wearing a dark T-shirt with a rhinestone spider web radiating outward across the front.

"It's only one long flight," I say. "Sometimes, if I happen to be here at just the right moment, I can find a neighbor to help. Otherwise, I can manage by myself."

The two women insist on carrying the stroller up the stairs for me. They are panting a little by the time we reach the apartment.

"This heat is killing me," the blond one says.

"Would you like to come in and have something cold to drink before you go?" I ask. "There's orange juice, Coke, anything you'd like."

"Water would be great."

They stand quietly outside the kitchen as I fill their glasses from the tap.

"This is super," says the blonde. "I mean, great water." She introduces herself, saying her name is Ice. "And this is Metro," she adds, gesturing toward her friend, who is staring at me and shaking her head so that the single star hanging from a chain in one earlobe swings from side to side.

144

"Never, ever wear a watch on your left hand," Metro says. "And I mean never."

"What?" I say.

"All of the energy from your body flows through your left arm," says Metro. "The watch will just absorb it all and leave you with nothing. I thought that was a commonly known fact."

"Maybe in some circles," I say, and surprise myself by contemplating, for only a moment, a switch to my other wrist.

"It has something to do with physics," Metro says. "Really." She moves a hand stiffly over her dark crew cut.

Ice sneezes quietly, almost politely, three times in a row. "I've been fighting a cold all day," she says. "Or maybe it's allergies."

"Yeah, well, everyone's fighting something," Metro says. "Colds, hay fever, personal demons, whatever." She is staring at me again, looking at me sharply, as if she doesn't like what she sees.

"Now what?" I say. "Don't tell me I'm wearing my shoes on the wrong feet."

"There are only two directions in life," Metro announces. "Toward the heart and away from the heart."

"Your baby's out of the stroller and into the garbage," Ice says. "I just thought I should point that out to you."

I scoot over to the plastic garbage pail, and fall to my knees next to Sarah, who is rolling a cigarette butt between her fingers. "Drop it," I say. She smiles at me lovingly, showing off all four teeth. Pitching the cigarette butt to the floor, she examines a peach pit carefully before putting it into her mouth.

"Cute baby!" Ice says. "I'd die for a baby like that."

Metro shrugs. "Would you mind if I used your bathroom?"

Walking to the kitchen doorway, I point down the hall.
Ice is behind me, her fingers laced around the middle of
her water glass. Like a bracelet, a bolt of blue lightning is
tattooed across one of her wrists.

"My husband has a tattoo," I say. "A little flowery thing
near his shoulder." I remember my shock at discovering
it the first time we undressed each other, so many years
ago in his dormitory room. I loved it that an accounting
student at Wharton had gone to a tattoo parlor in some
sordid part of Philadelphia and decorated himself with a
single, tiny long-stemmed rose. Newly in love, I wanted
to be amazed by him, to be taken by surprise. One night
in bed, a few months after we were married, I drew a
vase around his rose with a felt-tipped pen, added dai-
sies and lilies and a droopy-looking morning glory.
Bobby watched without a word as I drew, and there was
something about his silence that made me realize he'd
seen all of this before, that I was not the first who had
claimed him for my own. I stopped what I was doing and
went into the bathroom for a washcloth. I rubbed away
every bit of my work, rubbed away at his skin so fiercely
that Bobby cried out in pain. It was only when he seized
my hand and jerked it away from him that I finally gave
up.

"Oh, yeah?" Ice is saying. "So where *is* the lucky guy?"

I let out a long, noisy sigh that sounds like a whistle.
"Gone," I say.

"Bummer," says Ice, "but most of the time friends are
a whole lot better than family, anyway. They love you
and forgive you. Like Metro and myself. We fight but it's
not bad, not too serious."

Looking downward, I see that the baby is negotiating
her way between my legs and past me, heading up the
hallway to the living room, grabbing onto anything that
will make her passage easier—a door frame, the arm of
a couch, the edge of a table. She lets out a squeal of

happiness and races on her knees to the middle of the room, where a vast mountain of Bobby's belongings is covered by an orange Indian print bedspread. Rising five feet from the floor, under the bedspread, are all the things he left behind last summer: cartons of books and record albums; a lamp he made out of spare parts from his first MG; a file cabinet full of tearsheets clipped from *Car and Driver* and *Road & Track;* a porcelain sink attached to a white column that he'd been planning to make into a table; and a clay bust he had sculpted that failed as a self-portrait but turned out to bear a startling resemblance to Jesus Christ. God knows what else is under there—I haven't had the heart to take inventory since the day Bobby left, and, like a whirlwind, I gathered up his things and carried them off. I only got as far as the living room when exhaustion set in, and for all these months the mountain has stood there, ignored and almost forgotten. I barely even see it anymore. I vacuum around it, occasionally dusting off its peaks when the mood strikes me. Once, in the middle of a winter night, I dreamed that the mountain had simply vanished; awakening, I came out into the living room, heart thumping, and approached it in the dark. I settled myself at its foot, and drifted in and out of sleep, my head resting through the night on one of Bobby's cartons.

Ice circles the mountain with her hands held behind her back. "Jesus," she says respectfully. "Is this like, you know, modern art or something?"

"Hardly," I say, and swoop down over the baby, putting an end to her mountain-climbing. "It's just some junk that belongs down in Florida with my husband."

"Florida?" Emerging from the bathroom, Metro is rubbing her hands together, smoothing some of my cocoa butter across her knuckles. The sweet heavy scent of vanilla is overwhelming for a moment, almost sickening, and then it begins to fade.

"I was in Florida once," Metro reports cheerfully. "The sun was so hot it burned a hole right through my pocket."

I admire the slender fingers traveling soundlessly in circles along the back of Metro's hand. I notice another bolt of blue lightning across her wrist as well, and wonder if Metro and Ice are lovers. For some reason this frightens me, and I take a small step backward. But now Ice is leaning over me, bending to drop a tiny kiss high on my cheek.

"Thanks," she says.

"For what, a glass of water?" I say, sounding a little cranky.

"I mean, like, for your company," says Ice. "It was neat, wasn't it, to hang out and talk. People don't talk to each other enough. They go about their business, and that's that."

I nod my head. I see the tall, slightly stooped figure of my husband leaning against the kitchen table, hear his announcement that he's going off to Key West, going off to spend the rest of his life without me, but not alone. Why? I ask him, once, twice, and twice more. A few answers would be helpful, I say in a wobbly voice. And there is Bobby shrugging his shoulders, raising them almost to his ears and looking at me in surprise, as if he is just as surprised as I am, as if his astonishing betrayal is news to him, too. These things happen, he says, and strangely enough, in that moment he sounds like an ordinary man.

"Well, take it easy," I say now, seizing Ice's hands and then Metro's, pressing firmly against the bone and flesh of their cool fingers before closing the door behind them. In the kitchen, I rinse out their water glasses, fill the baby's bottle with apple juice, then take her with me into my steamy, sunlit bedroom, where I undress us both in slow motion. Sarah yawns gently as I lay her down along the middle of my bed for a nap. She sucks on her bottle, absently strokes the soft corners of my mouth, her eyes half-closed.

Leaving her there, I stand in my underwear in front of a gleaming rosewood dresser. I undo the leather clip at the back of my hair and watch as it falls in a deep-brown shawl past my shoulders. I reach into the dresser drawer for my silver-backed brush, an engagement gift from Bobby's grandmother. The brush is gone from the drawer, along with everything else left over from my marriage, and I let out a thin, sharp cry of pain, as if I had sliced into my finger with a razor. Everything— three or four gold bracelets, a string of silver beads, my wedding band. Gifts from another life, it seems, the one that slipped away from me so fast I didn't even notice it was already, impossibly, out of reach.

Metro, I say out loud. Senselessly, I look around for a note of apology or explanation.

These things happen, I hear Bobby saying, and I stare in disbelief as Metro helps herself to my gold and silver, her hands searching delicately through my things while Ice stands alongside me, close enough for a kiss.

Sounds

~~~~~~~~~~~~~~~~~~~~~~~~~~
~~~~~~~~~~~~~~~~~~~~~~~~~~

It's an enormous old house that my father and his new wife live in, at least by my standards. I was raised in a tract house in the suburbs of Philadelphia, with three tiny bedrooms crowded together on one floor, and not a single good hiding place anywhere. Here, the rooms are generous and high-ceilinged and fill three floors; it's a house that was once part of a plantation, built by slaves in another century. Nearly five years ago, Wes, my father, inherited this house in a small town in the deep South, but no money for its upkeep. Many of the interior walls are stained and peeling, and the outside hasn't been painted in years. But there are live oaks overhung with moss on the front lawn, and the sunsets over the water behind the property are miraculous.

"This is one lucky son-of-a-bitch you're looking at," my father says as I walk through the door with my suitcase. "Baby, I'm doing just great!" He spins around gracefully in his sneakers, snapping two fingers of each hand above his head like castanets.

"Don't be such a show-off," Janet teases. Meeting me for the first time, Janet's hands fly instantly to my shoulders. "Angela," she says, "let me look at you!" as if she'd last seen me when I was a child and couldn't get over how much I'd grown. I'm fond of her already, impressed by her composure, her warmth, the casual way she drapes an arm across my father's back.

Wes is in his early seventies. Janet is not quite thirty; in another life, we might have grown up together. The news of their marriage came in a phone call to me last summer. No big deal, really, Wes kept saying, sensing that I was close to tears, overcome by the simple fact that he had an enduring passion for someone I didn't even know. "Are you all right?" I heard my father say. "Your breathing sounds a little funny." When I did not respond he said, "It must be this long-distance connection, I guess." He was eager to talk, dying to, but I wasn't ready to listen to any of it. With my eyes closed, I imagined his lovesick face, the slightly goofy smile that lingered all day long. I hung up on him with my eyes still shut tight.

A few months ago, in the spring, Janet and Wes had a baby, and I can see now that my father is dizzy with happiness, strangely exhilarated by the sleepless nights and his daughter's endless demands.

"Wake that baby and I'll punch your lights out," Janet warns as he climbs the stairs with my suitcase. She leads me into the front parlor, where we sit on a worn velvet sofa and smile at each other without speaking. My father has described her as "a lovely big strong girl," a description that I wouldn't quarrel with. Janet is almost a head taller than I am, with large hands and long, square-tipped fingers. Under her faded denim maternity jumper, she is wearing a white T-shirt. Her ankles are crossed on a dark, heavy captain's chair, where she wiggles the toes of her bare feet. "I hope you'll stay for as long as you want," she says.

"Only a week," I say. Then it's back to Boston, where I'm a history instructor at a small, not very distinguished women's college.

"I'd love to live in Boston," Janet says. "Are you still with that guy who you bought the house with?"

I shake my head. "Seven years," I murmur. Looking down at Janet's still-wiggling toes, I say, "We'd just begun to wallpaper the bathroom ceiling, when I started to feel so closed-in, I could hardly breathe."

"Seven-year itch?" Janet asks. "Or was it just the smell of wallpaper paste?" I do not answer, and so Janet changes the subject and begins to talk about her life with Wes. She tells me that during the time they were living together in Philadelphia, before their marriage and move down South, she never quite got used to the idea that wherever they went, people were shamelessly curious about them. At first, when strangers would stare at them on the street or in a restaurant, Janet thought it was only her they were eyeing: that her bra strap was showing, her scarf was trailing in the mud, or that a wide streak of dirt was smeared along her cheek like a scar. But when friends came to visit and commented on how happy she and Wes seemed to be together, she'd become exasperated by the amazement in their voices.

I can see my father twirling in his white leather tennis shoes, hear the quick, sharp snap of his fingers. Trying to keep the amazement from my voice hasn't been easy. I can't understand the choices that Wes and Janet have made: They strike me as foolhardy, certain to lead to loss and grief. I feel the urge to shake Janet and say, "This isn't going to last; why do you keep pretending that it will?" I study her and imagine a young bewildered widow, raising a child by herself in this huge house that will seem overwhelming once Wes is gone.

Sighing out loud, I calculate how many years are left to my father's marriage.

"Hey you. Is that a standard sigh of longing I hear?" asks Wes. He steps into the parlor, with the baby in a seersucker pouch that is tied around his waist; a tiny, pleasant burden against her father's chest. "There's nothing like the birth of a baby to put things in proper perspective," Wes says. His face looks smooth and rosy, the face of a man who ages more gently than the rest of us, it seems. He isn't particularly tall, but his broad shoulders fill out a beautiful posture. Most of the time he dresses in tennis shoes, baggy corduroy pants, and denim work shirts with the sleeves rolled just past the elbows. (Why do you have to go around looking like such a slob, I can hear my mother saying mournfully. She lost that battle years ago, and then the whole war. When at last my father left her, with Janet waiting hungrily in the wings, my mother called me even before his car had pulled away from the curb. "It's over, thank God," she said. "It went on forever, didn't it, like a bad movie you can barely manage to sit through, but it's finally over." That evening, the two of us lay side by side in my parents' enormous bed, comforting each other through the night.)

I stroke the top of the baby's head with one finger. "Sweet pea," I say. "A very sweet baby."

"Actually, she looks a lot like you did at this age," Wes says. "Big eyes, and all that dark hair." I'm sure this is an outrageous lie, but I'm touched by it nevertheless.

"We have pictures of you to prove it," my father goes on. "I'd love to show them to you sometime."

"I believe you," I say unconvincingly.

"That's all right," says Wes. "A little skepticism is

always in order, no matter what the story. But let me run upstairs and get those pictures so you can see for yourself."

"I'd rather you didn't," I say. "Please."

"I *want* you to see them," Wes says. "You'd get a real kick out of them."

"Maybe so, but I just don't feel an overwhelming need to look at them right now."

"Come on, don't be such a coward," says Wes. "What are you afraid of?"

Janet seizes my father's wrist and yanks his arm back. "Why do you have to force yourself on her like that? Cut it out, Wes," she says. "I mean it."

Clicking his heels together, Wes says, "Yes, your royal madness." He does not watch her stalk from the parlor to the dining room to the kitchen, and is not jarred, as I am, when the swinging door at the entrance to the kitchen slams shut. "Sleep deprivation can be a terrible thing for some people," is all he says.

I am embarrassed for him, for all of us, and go back to stroking the baby's head. She is my half-sister, but I do not feel connected to her at all; in my mind, she is simply Janet's child, and could have been fathered by anyone.

"I never expected to find myself here," Wes says softly. "You know that, don't you?" My hand rests lightly, motionless now, on the baby's head. "When I was still married to your mother," Wes tells me, "my shrink kept saying, 'You cannot continue with this thing, you have absolutely *got* to let go of this young girl.' Ninety dollars an hour, and all I was doing was listening to a broken record. Normally, you know, they give you no advice whatsoever; they just lean back in their chairs and listen with their eyes closed. But in my case, the illustrious doctor felt the need to make an exception. He was so convinced that I was nuts, he just had to come right out and tell me so." Wes raises his arms in the air and lets out a deep, exuberant laugh. "And then comes the day when the goddamn fool of a pessimist doctor finally gives in and sends me a wedding present. A wedding present! A pair of glass candlesticks with a little card saying, 'Congratulations.'" My father is weeping with laughter. "Congrat-u-la-tions," he wheezes, one syllable at a time.

"Congratulations," I repeat. "Sorry it took me so long to get around to saying it."

The baby, Harper, has the hiccups. Suddenly calm, Wes jiggles her a bit in the pouch.

"Let her breathe into a paper bag," I joke, when she begins to whimper again.

"Here's my solution," says Wes, pretending he hasn't heard me. "This is a story my father used to tell me, which I am passing along to you, Harper. Ready? Once there was a little girl named Harper, whose father was always threatening to steal her nose. One day, when Harper least expected it, her father reached out and grabbed the nose right off her face. 'Daddy!' cried Harper. 'Give me my nose back right now.' She cried so pitifully that finally her father agreed to give it back. But when he did, he made one mistake: He put the nose back upside down. Too late! The nose was there to stay. Actually, it wasn't such a terrible thing after all. Except when it rained. 'Daddy!' Harper cried pitifully. 'The rain is falling straight down into my nose!' 'Stop your crying, Harper,' said her father. 'I have the perfect solution.' And in his hand was the tiniest umbrella anyone had ever seen. He glued it over Harper's nose, and father and daughter lived forever after in peace and harmony."

I applaud; the baby's hiccups have disappeared, but now she is screaming.

"Hungry, I bet," says Wes. "Angela, go into the kitchen and get a bottle from Janet, please."

I'm off, sliding in my socks to the kitchen along bare varnished floors, thinking that I envy this baby, this child of my father's old age, and that it's probably true Wes won't be around long enough for either of them to have an opportunity to disappoint the other.

In the kitchen, Janet is seated at a butcher-block table deveining a large pile of shrimp on a sheet of newspaper. Her long dark hair is in a high ponytail that just reaches the back of her neck. "Miserable work," she says mildly. "It's so hot and humid in here. I wish we could afford to put in air-conditioning."

"It's a wonderful house," I say, sitting down beside her. "People would kill for a house like this." Beyond the window, the water in the bay swishes against a small dock.

"I really need to get back to work," she says. I stare at her hands slicing into the silvery shrimp. "I mean real work." Janet free-lances as an artist for a greeting card company. Her drawings are very appealing; beautifully detailed animals living like humans—elephants reading in bed, pandas cooking Chinese food in a wok, geese in tuxedos and formal gowns on the dance floor. She started out as a portrait painter, eventually switching to greeting cards to help pay the bills. My father, of course, is retired. So the house is steamy all summer long and probably a bit chilly in winter. This is the life you chose, I want to tell her. Instead I say, "The courage this marriage takes just overwhelms me."

Knife in hand, Janet balances her chair on two legs, then falls forward. "The truth is, I'm not very brave," she says, her voice close to a whisper. "It's the loneliness, I guess, that I can't seem to get used to. There's no one for me here, no one I can really connect with, just a lot of friends Wes inherited from his brother—older people I speak to politely, smiling and nodding my head, hoping they won't notice that I'm saying nothing at all."

"The baby." I shoot up from my seat as if an alarm had sounded. "My father sent me in for a bottle."

"Wes is so happy," says Janet, going to the refrigerator and choosing a bottle wedged between jars of mayonnaise and mustard. She holds it under a flow of hot water at the sink—water so hot it steams. Her head is tipped back, and she drinks from the nipple for a moment, very casually. "Good enough," she says, handing the bottle to me. Then, "This is the happiest time of his life, I think. I wouldn't ask him to part with any of it— the house, his friends, the contentment he feels just wandering from room to room, smiling because it's all his."

Wes is racing toward us, Harper bouncing gently against his chest. He frees her from the pouch, grabs the bottle from me, and pokes it into the baby's mouth. "Talk talk talk," he says, smiling. "You ladies really know how to yack it up." Delicately, with his free hand, he raises Janet's ponytail and kisses the back of her neck, where a thin gold chain gleams. "Keep right on talking," he says. "Pretend I'm merely a bystander, innocently minding my own business." He winks at us, pleased with what he has found: two women sharing secrets in a kitchen lighted with late-afternoon sun. "I know when I'm not wanted," he says, pretending to be insulted. Shoulders hunched, head drooping extravagantly, he retreats from us.

"I'm beginning to feel," says Janet, the moment he is gone from the kitchen, "as if I've lost my way; as if I can't see where I'm going anymore. Sometimes I imagine I'm holding a map of my life in my hands, and my fingers are traveling along those spidery lines to see if they will take me exactly where they promised." She looks past me dreamily, her face polished with perspiration. "You know where I could find one of those?"

There's a light knock at the door next to the pantry, and a curly-haired man with bloodshot eyes appears, followed by a cocker spaniel limping close behind, one of its hind legs encased in a plaster cast. The man, whose face is sunburned and handsome, beams at Janet. He looks me over, and apparently deciding I am harmless, plants a silent kiss on Janet's mouth.

"Ah," breathes Janet, taking a nervous step backward, nearly losing her balance and falling into the white brick fireplace that is next to the refrigerator. "Matt," she says, "this is Wes's daughter."

"Wes's daughter," says Matt slowly. He strokes the underside of his neck, and narrows his eyes. "No problem," he says. "I can deal with it." He lifts the cocker spaniel into his lap and absently drapes one of its beautiful silk ears over his own mouth. The plaster cast on the dog's leg is decorated with autographs, I notice, and I bend down for a closer look. "It's a dog's life!" someone has written in tiny green letters, and "Hope to see you back on the dance floor soon!"

"What happened?" I ask Matt.

"What happened?" he repeats, his voice muffled behind the dog's ear. "What happened was a miracle. My life was empty, romantically speaking, as empty as . . . the shelves of my linen closet before my trip to the Laundromat—"

"Enough," Janet says sharply.

"The dog," I say, tapping my finger against the plaster cast.

"You mean Napoleon?" says Matt. "Napoleon is a crime victim—a clear case of hit and run."

Janet is standing over the stove, checking on the shrimp boiling in a blackened cast-iron pot. Right below the knob of bone at the beginning of her spine there's a chip of diamond encircled in gold—a part of the necklace that had been hidden before. I picture my father fastening this gift around her neck, then dropping back to admire her. We're doing just great, aren't we, he tells her. Better than anyone could have imagined.

Taped over the fireplace is an unframed print by Paul

Klee. I drift toward it, away from Janet and Matt. I study
a pair of cartoonlike figures holding fishing rods; between the men and the fish beneath them floats an ex-
clamation mark. The print is entitled "They're Biting,"
and for some reason it makes me laugh. I think of Matt's
head lowering to drop his silent kiss, and crazily, my
shoulders begin to tremble. In a moment, I am laughing
out loud, crossing my arms against my chest, as if I were
trying to contain the laughter inside it. "Are you staying
for dinner?" I hear Janet ask. Listening hard for Matt's
response, my laughter vanishes.

"As a matter of fact," says Matt, "I haven't eaten since
breakfast."

"Stay," says Janet, and I'm not fooled for a minute:
This is a woman who sees, with no effort at all, precisely
where she is going.

"So how are you doing these days, Matt," says Wes
cheerfully, smiling at him from one end of the oval dining table. Janet is at the other end, far from her husband; Matt and I are seated opposite one another. "How
are things going down at the Pick 'N Save?"

"Not terribly exciting," says Matt. "Sometimes I fall
asleep at the counter."

"Matt works at one of the markets in town," says Wes.
"He's a whiz at the cash register, fingers flying across that
little electronic keyboard."

"I'd rather not talk about that part of my life," Matt
says, and collects a few grains of rice from his plate with
a fingertip. "It makes me seem so unexceptional."

"Really," says Wes. "And what part of your life would
you like to talk about?" The smile on his face is broad; he
holds it in place so long, I can see the ends of his mouth
quivering. Matt leans away from his seat, softly calling
Napoleon's name until finally the dog emerges from

under the table, licks the rice from Matt's finger, then limps away.

"I once worked in a Seven-Eleven," Janet offers quickly. "The place was robbed so often, the manager used to stick the money from his own wallet inside a plastic head of lettuce he kept at the back of the soda case. 'Lett-Us-Hide,' it was called." Janet continues talking, listing job after job she'd held to supplement the income from her painting. But I'm no longer listening carefully. I'm too busy holding my breath, watching my father as if he were hanging from a trapeze, about to risk everything as he contemplates an extravagant series of somersaults in midair.

"Far out," I hear Matt say. "You really worked at a women's prison? What were they in for?"

"Drugs, mostly," says Janet, and Wes and I laugh as Matt's face goes dead-white. Wes reaches for his wallet, snaps it open, flashes his Social Security card.

"FBI," he says. "You're under arrest."

Matt glares at him.

Wes is completely still for a moment. Then, with a dramatic sweep of his arm, he lifts his water glass from the table. "To us," he says, looking all around him, nodding at each of us in turn. "To family, friends..." His voice trails off to a murmur.

"To us," we answer quietly, and slip the stems of our glasses through our fingers. There is the sound of glass against glass, of water delicately sipped. Under the table, the dog sighs, sounding wistful.

It is a little after 2:00 A.M.; the night air, through a second-story bedroom window, is drier now, carrying only the faintest scent of the Atlantic. Lying on a canopied bed, with a mattress half the size I'm used to, I listen as Harper cries steadily across the hall, one urgent, high-pitched wail after another. Footsteps fall lightly outside my room—probably Janet's. I think of her and Wes trooping up the stairs to bed tonight with their arms inexplicably laced around each other, confusing me with their tenderness. After dinner, when Matt had gone, his plate was cleared from the table, washed and put away, as if he had never been there at all but had only been imagined. Perhaps promises have been exchanged in whispers above my head, and my father's marriage has become a simple affair, easy to read. Husband, wife, and child, bound by love, presumably forever. Perhaps that is how it has appeared to Wes and Janet all along.

Once, I remember, my father had a close friend who was a very successful marriage counselor. He lived in the suburbs but slept at his office in Philadelphia three or four evenings a week, saying he needed to see clients late into the night. He was happily married; his wife drove a silver Ferrari he had given her, and had no complaints. "You don't know," my father had insisted when I said it all sounded unlikely, even ludicrous. "You can't even guess at how far people are willing to go to make room for each other."

Maybe so.

Needing to move about, knowing I will never fall back asleep, I travel down the stairs, a thin satin-edged blanket flowing behind me. In the front parlor, I search for the light switch and slouch against the sofa, my legs drawn up on the velvet cushions.

"What brings you to this part of town?" a voice says. I look up: My father stands in the center of the room in faded pajamas, tennis shoes, and a Phillies baseball cap, the brim facing sideways. An empty baby bottle is tucked under one arm.

"Do you always sleep in a baseball cap?" I ask.

"I just put the baby down in her crib. Come into the kitchen and keep me company while I fix some bottles for the morning. With so many dinner guests tonight, I forgot about them completely." I follow him into the kitchen and watch as he tears off what looks like a miniature see-through sandwich bag from a dispenser, then curves it around the inside of a hollow plastic bottle. He does this masterfully, repeating the process three times, filling the bottles with a yellowish formula that he pours from a large tin can. "Pretty impressive for an old guy, what do you think?" he says. Pushing the bottles aside, he perches on top of the counter and smiles at me. "Fairy tales can come true, It could happen to you..." he sings. My father flaps his hands from side to side, keeping time with his singing.

"Right you are," I say.

"How about strolling over here and sitting next to me?" Slowly I walk toward him, and raise myself onto the counter. "Now look me in the eye," he orders.

Instantly, I shut my eyes.

"You think I'm an old fool," my father says. "Say it."

Eyes wide open now, I grab my father's hands. He turns his palms upward, waiting for me to read his fortune. "You're no different from anyone else," I say. Tears fill my throat; I lean back against my father and feel his arms close around me.

"It's just that there's so little time," he whispers in my ear, soft as a secret.

Amazing: Here I am giving away secrets to a cab driver, a thin, cheerless teenage girl who isn't the least bit impressed with my news.

"It's been three years since I've seen my father," I tell her again as she lets me off at the bottom of the endless unpaved driveway that leads to my father's house. "Years," I say.

The driver turns halfheartedly around. "Take it easy," is all she says.

Striding across the wide lawn with a vinyl flight bag slung over my shoulder, I hear the small, distant sound of a horn blowing somewhere. When at last I reach the steps that lead to the open porch, I recognize, from an envelope of snapshots, my father's little girl. She's standing barefoot on the top stair, a tiny figure blowing a toy trumpet with two red ribbons hanging down from it. "Hey, you guys," she yells. "Hey, you guys." Behind her are Janet and Wes. This is only the second time that the two of us have met, and although I like Janet well enough, I still find the idea of their marriage a little hard to take. And so I have been content, these past three years, with the simple exchange of gifts and photographs and telephone calls at all the appropriate moments. I've come South on an insufferably hot summer day because my father, always miraculously young and healthy, has not been well in months. "Come and see for yourself," Janet had urged me over the phone, sounding impatient and impossibly weary. "I don't have the heart to explain to people what just can't be explained."

She is smiling at me now from the porch, saying how happy they are that I've made the trip.

"Me, too," I say, head tilted upward so our eyes can meet, at least for an instant or two. My father is standing, leaning his weight against her, his face entirely slack, his look sweetly childlike and somewhat dazed. Climbing the last step, I rush forward, wrap my arms around him, and wait for his embrace. His mouth opens. "Ah," he drawls, and it comes out sounding like a cry of pain, or ecstasy, perhaps. His arms hang limply, uselessly, at his sides, and I see that Janet is actually holding him up, that without her he would pitch forward and topple to the porch floor.

My chin rests on his shoulder and my hands travel up

and down his sides, counting ribs. "Ah," my father says directly into my ear. "Ah."

"Angela?" says Janet. "He's saying your name, Angela."

"Daddy?" Harper says. "Daddy and Mommy, Mommy and Daddy, I'm going to wash the car now, okay?"

At nearly three and a half, she's a pretty blonde with thick ankles and a mouth full of tiny perfect teeth. The last time I saw her, she was a dark-haired baby who rode about in a pouch tied tightly around my father's waist.

"You're so grown up," I tell her, withdrawing from my father and dropping to my knees next to Harper. "Do you have a driver's license yet?" This is my half-sister I'm down here on the floor trying to woo, I suddenly realize, and the sadness of this makes me laugh out loud. "I have a present for you," I say. "Right here in my bag."

Expertly, Harper opens the zipper and empties the contents onto the floor piece by piece, ignoring the little wrapped package entirely. It is a bright blue plastic cylinder of deodorant that interests her most, and without uncapping it, she rubs the hard plastic vigorously under each arm. "Can I have this?" she says, and runs off with it down the stairs.

I collect my things and put them back in the bag. "Don't worry about it," I say.

"I'm sorry," says Janet. She walks my father into the house and settles him into an armchair in the front parlor where I collapse at his feet noiselessly. "Lemonade?" Janet says. "Perrier? I'll be back in a minute." She is barefoot and dressed in shorts and a sleeveless pink-and-white striped blouse whose armholes are ringed with perspiration. I stare at her blackened heels as she abandons us.

My father begins to talk, but all I hear are sounds, a language of ahs and oohs and occasionally a consonant, which I seize upon excitedly, as if it were a clue that might lead to something important. My father loves to talk, has always loved to talk, and has always been happiest, at his most expansive, when he's surrounded by people who will listen to him.

But it's just the two of us now in this steamy, high-ceilinged parlor filled with heavy, worn furniture, just the two of us smiling away at each other, embarrassed at our helplessness.

"Ah," my father says, and his smile broadens. "Wow."

"You're so happy to see me?" I say. "You want me to know how happy you are that I'm here?"

"No."

"You're not happy to see me?"

"No, no." My father talks for a while, guesses that I'm not following him, smiles, and shakes his head. He looks over at the mantelpiece, covered in blistering paint and crowded with family snapshots. I spring from the floor and rush to the fireplace, gathering up the photographs in a frenzy.

"No," my father says, still looking toward the mantel. I notice a pair of wire-rimmed eyeglasses lying open between some picture frames and bring them to him triumphantly.

"On," he says, and I lower them onto his nose, curve the side pieces behind his ears. Exhausted, I sink to the floor again. My father begins to utter one shapeless, ill-defined sound after another, racing to tell me everything he knows.

I shake my head, shrug my shoulders, letting him know that I am lost.

"Ah," he says, and sighs sympathetically.

I think of my mother, who, a few years ago, still had enough energy to hate my father on her deathbed. I wonder if the sound of his voice now would have softened her, or if she would have pointed a finger at Janet, saying, *This is the life you chose, sweetie.*

No—that was me at my worst, keeping the words to myself but turning them over in my head a hundred times.

I see that my father has read my mind. His speech is agitated and rapid, and there is a tear at the corner of one eye. "Ah!" he shouts.

"I haven't been listening, I'm sorry."

"No." There is something more he wants me to do, that much I understand. "Ahm." He looks into his lap.

"Arms?" His arms are at his sides, jammed between the chair and his thighs, just where Janet left them. "You want me to move them for you?"

"Yah," he says matter-of-factly.

I kneel in front of him and reach for an arm. It's flaccid in my hands, the muscle gone, the skin startlingly cool against my fingers. Delicately I arrange one arm and then the other in his lap, as if I were arranging flowers. I lace the fingers of his left hand through the right and step back to search my father's smiling face. "Ah," he coos. I lay my head in his lap and imagine his hand coming down slowly over the slope of my skull, falling sweetly through my hair. "Ah," he croons. I tell him about my life, about the man I'm in love with, about my teaching job in New York. I talk and talk, endlessly, making up for lost time. My father comments here and there, and I'm quick to agree with him, eager to pretend that suddenly, miraculously, I've learned to read his mysterious sounds.

"Hey you guys," Harper bellows without warning.

"Ha," my father says, dragging out the syllable, filling it with warmth. "Ha."

I lift my head, and see that Harper is carrying a big mud-spattered toy truck in one hand and an exceptionally thin, grayish blanket in the other. She looks at me in a friendly way and says, "Move, please."

"I was just leaving anyway," I tell her, and, rising, step

to the side. Bustling about noisily, she drags an ottoman across the floor to my father, then waits for him to put up his feet. She carefully arranges her blanket across his legs like a tablecloth, then crawls underneath with her truck, saying, "Bye you guys."

My father smiles. "Joo," he says a few moments later.

"She's the joy of your life?" I say.

"No."

"It's so clear, anyone can see it."

"No. Joo."

"I'm on the wrong track entirely?" Unexpectedly, I break into laughter, thinking of the game Password and wondering what prize may be coming my way if only I can get things right.

Confused by my laughter, my father shakes his head. "Joo!" he says. *Joo, you idiot.*

"Juice," says a voice from under the blanket. "He wants juice."

"Good going, Harper," I say, relieved and grateful. "I'm so bad at this."

"So bad at what?" Janet says, arriving empty-handed and dressed in a new outfit—baggy white pants, a clean white T-shirt, short white leather boots decorated with fringes and shiny colored stones. "I forgot the drinks but I remembered the dinner, which, in fact, is almost ready."

My father is saying something to me now, and I watch Janet watching his face, listen as she skillfully smooths out the syllables, the poor misshapen words he strings together for me.

"You tried so hard," Janet translates. "I love it that you tried so hard.... You were funny, hopping around, a little panicky, wanting to do well...."

"Funny?" I say. "How could you see it that way?"

"Don't look so sad," Janet translates as my father goes on. "Get over here and give me a kiss."

But it is Janet I am walking toward, as if in a daze, Janet whose ear receives my noisy awkward kiss.

"Oh, Angela," she says, and in that "oh" is the pitch-dark sound of the hard, mean struggle that has become her life.

"No," says my father. He shakes his head, seeing that I've got it all wrong.

At the kitchen table, a long wooden rectangle painted mint-green, I cut my father's dinner into miniature squares. Across the room, at the counter, Janet is doing the same for Harper. We are alone and work in silence, concentrating hard, the quiet chatter of knives and forks against china so sweetly familiar.

Now Janet is talking, telling me that one by one their friends in town have fallen away. "You can't really blame them," she says, without much bitterness. "You can see how overwhelming it would be for most people."

My gaze settles on the bright-colored stones that orna-ment her boots. "I like your emeralds and rubies," I say.

"Aren't they great?" Janet matches her ankles together and lifts her toes off the floor. "You know how every now and then you come across something that you've got to have, that you just can't pass up, no matter what the cost?"

I think of Janet's lover, Matt, a handsome, spaced-out Looney Tune, who had shared dinner with us the last time I was here. My father knew him for what he was and seemed not to care, or not to love Janet any less because of him. All of this was the worst kind of news to me, but my father, I saw, was able to make do. Knowing what to take seriously and what to ignore—perhaps that's the gift that's kept him young.

"Matt," I hear myself say out loud.

"What?"

"I was wondering," I say in a tiny voice, "if he was still in the picture."

Janet is hunched over Harper's dinner, cutting fiercely into roast beef; both of us wince as her knife goes out of control and screeches across the plate. "He was around at just the right moment," she says calmly. "He was needy and so was I, that's all."

"And now?"

"You must be out of your mind," Janet says, "if you think I would pull that on Wes now. Really."

For what feels like a long while, I fool with my father's dinner, arranging the squares of food into an abstract mosaic of red and green. "You probably want to punch me," I say finally. "I can understand that."

Janet shrugs. "It's already forgotten," she says, and goes off to the parlor in search of her husband and daughter.

"I don't want this," Harper says when her plate is set in front of her. "I want soolami. And eggs. I don't want this."

"That's tomorrow," Janet says. "Tonight is roast beef." She scoots her chair around to my father's side, tucks a long trail of paper toweling into the round neck of his shirt.

Harper begins to cry.

"I know it's difficult," Janet says, "not getting what you want just when you want it, but that's the way it is some-times, sweetness." Feeding my father bits of meat and tomato and lettuce, she looks over her shoulder at Harper. "You *like* roast beef," she says.

"I know," Harper sobs.

"Ha," my father calls out to her. "Ha."

Climbing down from her seat, Harper pushes her way between Janet and Wes, making room for herself in her father's lap, jolting her mother's arm so that a forkful of food drops to the floor.

"You may not sit here while I'm feeding Daddy," Janet says. "Off."

"Feed *me*," Harper says. "I'm a baby, too."

"Wrong," says Janet. "I need you to be the biggest and best girl you can possibly be."

"*I* need to put a tape in the VCR," Harper announces. "My *Wee Sing* tape." She slips away from the table and out of the room, and quickly Janet rises, preparing to go after her.

"Do you know what the worst of it is?" she asks us. "I spend half my life cutting up food into smaller and smaller pieces that no one cares enough to even taste."

"Uh oh," my father warns, and continues on, leaving me behind, a backward child who can't understand the simplest thing. I listen to them arguing, to Janet insisting, "I *do* mean it, goddamn it, why do you keep saying I don't?" The next moment she is slamming out of the room and I'm easing into her seat, settling in at my father's side.

"You know," I say, my voice low and hesitant as I lift a forkful of tomato to my father's lips, "you know, I had a dream the other night that Mommy came back for a quick visit, expressly for the purpose of organizing my closets. Unfortunately, she only had time to do the one in the foyer before she had to go back, but she did a wonderful job—she even managed to fit in the vacuum cleaner and the ironing board so that they didn't both fall on top of you when you opened the closet door. You can imagine how disappointed I was when I woke up and realized it was only a dream."

My father is staring at me in utter astonishment, unable to speak at all. "In my mind she was so pure," I say shamelessly. "She always smelled good and her handwriting was perfect." It occurs to me that I could go on like this forever, that I have never felt so powerful in my life. I look at my father's swollen wrists, at the swollen fingers of his hands that lie so patiently in his lap. I see him three years ago, showing off his new life, snapping his fingers high above his head, hear him boasting good-naturedly, "Baby, I'm doing just great!" I hear the bright snap of his fingers, the clear sharp sound of unexpected happiness.

"Ah," my father is saying now. "Ah," he says urgently.

"Are you all right?" I ask, half-wanting to apologize but happy enough to get away without it.

"Up."

"You want me to help you up?"

"Yah."

"Okay, you tell me what to do."

My father laughs at this, as if I've already been forgiven. "Eee," he says.

"It's easy?"

"Yah."

Standing in front of him, I reach for his arms: Over and over again, I seize his cool, smooth flesh, which begins to grow warm and moist at my frantic touch. After every effort to pull him up, he falls back against his seat, exhausted and disappointed. I think of all the ways, real and imagined, that we have failed each other over the years. It is this simplest of failures, to raise him out of a hard-backed kitchen chair, that seems unforgivable now as I let go in defeat.

"What are you *doing?*" Janet cries out to me, just in time to see my father flop back into his chair. "What's the matter with you?" She makes her way to the table in a panicky rush, Harper close behind her, echoing, "What's the matter with you guys?"

"Up," says my father, and explains, I suppose, exactly what went wrong.

Afterward, Janet touches my shoulder lightly. "It only

172

seems like the end of the world," she says. "But believe me, it's not even close." She stands behind my father and places her hands directly under his armpits.

"One," my father says.

"Two...three," Janet and Harper say together in the same soft voice, and I watch as Janet lifts him so lovingly and with such ease, out of his chair and into the perfect shelter of her arms.

"Wow," my father says. His gaze travels from me to Janet and then back to me again. He speaks just a few words now, each offered up to me generously, in slow motion, in his own impossible language.

"There's so much to say," Janet translates, and the half-smile at her lips is full of my father's longing.

ABOUT THE AUTHOR

Marian Thurm has published fiction in *The New Yorker, The Atlantic, Redbook, Mademoiselle, The Boston Globe Magazine,* and many other magazines. Her work has been chosen for several anthologies, including *Best American Short Stories,* edited by Anne Tyler, and *Editor's Choice.* Her first novel, *Walking Distance,* was published in 1987, and a collection of her stories, *Floating,* was published in 1984. Ms. Thurm is a graduate of Vassar College and of Brown University, and lives in New York City with her husband and two young children.